He was a stranger. And she didn't care....

Jillian didn't care what it took, she was going to get her sister back. She'd lie, steal—do anything she had to. Where was her sister right now? What was happening to her? And what would happen to her—to the other women, too—once the truck reached its destination? As much as Jillian wanted to block out the obvious, she couldn't.

Halfway down the stairs, her vision blurred. Her chest tightened. She couldn't breathe. Another few steps and she plopped down hard, tears starting to flow unchecked. She wiped at them with both hands. She couldn't afford to break down now. Tears didn't solve a damn thing.

When warm hands grasped her shoulders, she jerked as if to escape, and then she realized it was Rick. She turned and plunged blindly into his arms. He caught her, his arms closing tightly around her.

LORI L. HARRIS

TAKEN

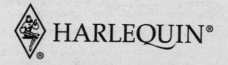

HARLEQUIN®

TORONTO • NEW YORK • LONDON
AMSTERDAM • PARIS • SYDNEY • HAMBURG
STOCKHOLM • ATHENS • TOKYO • MILAN • MADRID
PRAGUE • WARSAW • BUDAPEST • AUCKLAND

ISBN-13: 978-0-373-69277-4
ISBN-10:   0-373-69277-3

TAKEN

ABOUT THE AUTHOR

Lori L. Harris has always enjoyed competition. She grew up in southern Ohio, showing Arabian horses and Great Danes. Later she joined a shooting league where she competed head to head with police officers—and would be competing today if she hadn't discovered how much fun and challenging it was to write. Romantic suspense seemed a natural fit. What could be more exciting than writing about life-and-death struggles that include sexy, strong men?

When not in front of a computer, Lori enjoys remodeling her home, gardening and boating. Lori lives in Orlando, Florida, with her very own hero.

Books by Lori L. Harris

HARLEQUIN INTRIGUE
830—SOMEONE SAFE
901—TARGETED*
907—SECRET ALIBI*
1010—TAKEN

*The Blade Brothers of Cougar County

CAST OF CHARACTERS

Jillian Sorensen—After fifteen years away, she's coming home to Charleston, South Carolina, to confront her past. But one wrong turn on a remote road and Jillian must face something far more terrifying than past demons.

Rick Brady—He has his own agenda, and it's to find his father's killer. He'll use whatever measures are necessary—even the beautiful and tenacious Jillian Sorensen. But in order to do so, he'll have to get her to trust him first.

Megan Sorensen—Jillian's adopted sister. Jillian has always fought Megan's battles for her, so in her darkest hours, Megan trusts Jillian not to let her down.

Jim Brady—Eight years ago, he was the lead investigator for one of Charleston's most horrific crimes—The Midnight Run Murders. It was the one case that this seasoned detective could never walk away from. Even in retirement.

Debra Wert—She's the unknown face that will become the task force's first break. And maybe the killer's next victim.

Randy Gardner—Who hired him to kill Jillian? And when he died, why did he have Jim Brady's notebook in his pocket?

Detective Nate Langley—This Charleston County detective has no problem closing cases. But is his most recent one connected to the Midnight Run Murders?

Special Agent Thomas Durwood—He's one of the FBI's best field agents. But is he good enough to save Megan Sorensen and the other victims?

Sheriff Ben Tanner—He's New Carlyle County, Pennsylvania's sheriff and a family man.

Chapter One

"So. Are we lost?" Taking her eyes off the dark road, Jillian Sorensen glanced over at her sister.

They'd left Cincinnati at eight that morning amid snow flurries, but as they'd traveled south through North Carolina the temperature had climbed into the lower seventies—balmy by Ohio standards—and they'd lowered the convertible top.

Megan studied the road map a bit too intently. "Well?" Jillian prompted.

"That depends."

Jillian tried to capture the strand of hair that had worked loose from her ponytail. Taking a deep breath, she spoke again. "Megan? What's the map say?"

Without looking up, Megan rotated the map beneath the flashlight beam. "Say? Were you expecting it to talk?"

"I figure the chance of it speaking is roughly the same as your being able to read it."

The beginnings of a frown formed on Megan's face. "Keep it up…"

"Come on." Jillian felt her already depleted patience hit rock bottom. "After thirteen hours behind the wheel, I want out of this car for more than the few minutes it takes to eat a meal or fill up the gas tank. Getting lost in a national forest isn't on my agenda."

"Then you're not going to like hearing this." Megan gave a slight shrug. A bad sign. "We're on US 17A instead of US 17."

"How—"

"Doesn't matter," Megan cut her off. "It's no biggie. There should be a shortcut coming up here pretty quickly." In an effort to read the small print, she held the map closer to her face. "It looks like County Road 45."

"Looks like?" Jillian slowed. "Show me."

Just as Megan thrust the map forward, the flashlight flickered and then died. Dropping the map and the light, Megan pointed at the road ahead instead. "There's a sign. Highway 45. Do you see it on the left?"

Jillian made the turn, but then glanced over at her sister. "You're absolutely sure about this?"

"Trust me."

"You said that the last time you got us lost."

To keep it from being blown away, Megan shoved the folded map down between her seat and the center console. "We weren't lost."

"That's not what you told that military cop when we ended up in a restricted area."

"That was different." Megan grinned. "He was really cute. And big, tough military types like defenseless women. I got a date out of it, didn't I?"

Jillian wordlessly adjusted her hands on the steering

wheel as she tried to think of a good comeback. The guy really had been cute, though. And nice.

"Stop worrying." Megan fumbled with the earbuds for her iPod. "This road takes us back to US 17." She rested her head against the seat and closed her eyes. "We'll be in Charleston by midnight. You'll get plenty of sleep before the big job interview."

For the briefest of moments, as Jillian glanced over at her adoptive sister, she didn't see the graceful twenty-one-year-old woman sitting beside her now. Instead she saw the eleven-year-old child Megan had been the year Jillian had gotten her driver's license. She recalled how Megan's blond pigtails had bounced in a summer breeze, the way her smile had spread wide, the way her eyes had looked at Jillian with trust and certainty.

Megan had been the first person to trust Jillian, to really trust her. And after nearly seven years in foster care, Jillian had been desperate for approval—even from a child.

The Sorensens, her adopted family, had given Jillian something she'd never expected to have. A sense of safety. Of love. Of being part of something bigger than herself. For the first time in her life, she had felt lucky.

"You're doing it again." Opening one eye, Megan looked at Jillian.

"I'm doing what again?"

"Watching me. As if you think I'm going to fall apart again."

Five weeks ago, less than forty-eight hours after their father's funeral, Megan had come home drunk for what she'd sworn was the first time in her life. Three nights later Jillian had found her passed out on the bathroom floor.

With both parents now dead and no other family, it had been up to Jillian to confront her sister about the drinking.

She'd said some really harsh things that had left their relationship somewhat strained.

"I was not watching you."

Megan turned in her seat. "Yes. You were. And I'm fairly certain that's why you're interviewing with Burroughs, Alderson & Bailey. Because you think I need looking after."

"That's not true. It's a great opportunity."

"Maybe for someone who is interested in practicing corporate law." Megan gave her a sharp look.

Jillian met her gaze briefly. "And your point is?"

"For the past year, all you've talked about is going into a family law practice. Helping women and children." Megan straightened in her seat again. "You've been playing big sister for a lot of years, Jilly. Maybe it's time to give it a rest."

"That's not what I'm doing."

"Sure it is. The only reason you're even considering this job is because it's in Charleston. Where I'll be going to medical school."

"Yeah," Jillian agreed dryly. "That's my only incentive for taking a position with a really prestigious firm at a starting salary nearly double what the others are offering." She held a hand up in the air. "And it also has nothing to do with how much I hate Ohio winters."

"I just don't want you taking it because you're worried about me, okay? I know that I've been making some dumb decisions recently, but all that's behind me. I'm perfectly capable of being on my own. I wish you'd believe me."

The plaintive note in Megan's voice deflated Jillian's frustration. "I do believe you. Maybe I'm the one who's not ready to be alone. There, I admitted it. Happy?"

"Yeah." Megan's smile returned, easing the remaining tension. She pointed ahead to where their headlights flashed on a sign in the distance. Both women focused on it as they drew closer.

"Next right, Hellhole Bay." Megan read the sign aloud. "Sounds like a real tourist destination. Should we stop?"

"Maybe on the return trip."

The road took a quick, sharp turn, seeming to narrow. Tall trees on either side pressed up from the pavement, forming a canyon. Jillian watched the moonlight chase after them, its light flooding down like a stage spot through the occasional wide openings in the canopy. Then suddenly the hammock of oaks and pines grew too dense. Too dark.

Because of the surrounding woods, the rhythmic rumble of the engine became louder and the air turned even cooler.

Megan pulled a jacket from behind Jillian's seat. "What do you think about putting up the top?"

Jillian shook her head, then shivered. It wasn't just because of the sudden drop in temperature, though. "To be honest, I'd rather not stop out here." They hadn't passed a single car in the past fifteen minutes.

Megan, who had already shoved one arm into a sleeve, looked up from where she was struggling to locate the second one. "Are you afraid some man is lurking in the woods?" Having found the sleeve opening, she tugged the coat in place. "Just waiting for a car to come along and break down so he can use a machete on the driver and female passenger?"

Her sister's description of a scene from the slasher movie they'd rented two nights ago left Jillian feeling slightly ridiculous. "Actually—" she fought the urge to grin "—I was only worried about the driver."

Folding her arms across her, Megan tried to pretend she was affronted, but Jillian knew better.

"So you're suggesting that you'd just leave me on the side of the road with some crazed killer?"

"I wouldn't even look in the rearview mirror."

Megan zipped the jacket. "Okay. You win. Pull over. Given the fact that I haven't stopped shivering since we made that turn back there, I'm willing to risk death."

"It's your neck." Jillian had started to shift her foot off the accelerator and toward the brake when a person—a woman—suddenly exploded from the trees and into the convertible's path.

The woman looked up, frozen in the headlights.

Bracing her hands against the dash, Megan screamed.

As Jillian stood on the brakes, everything seemed to slow—not just inside her head, but around her, too. It was as if the woman waited at the end of a well-lit tunnel. Pale hair. Pale skin.

But it was the look in her eyes—the calm acceptance of what was about to happen—that shocked Jillian. Did she want to die?

And then, at the last moment, the woman looked over her shoulder, as if searching for some way to escape the inevitable. Jillian jerked the wheel to the right to avoid hitting the woman.

Megan screamed again, the sound catapulting Jillian back into real time as the tires lost traction. The passenger-side tires dropped off the asphalt and immediately ran over something—a log or a rock.

The impact ripped the steering wheel from her hands. By the time she grabbed it again, the car was sliding sideways and she no longer looked out through the windshield where passing tree trunks whizzed by like an unending barcode, but was staring into her sister's panicked eyes.

And then, just as suddenly, the convertible was rocking hard from side to side as it settled on its tires facing back the way they'd just come from. Throwing Jillian and Megan around one last time.

For several seconds both women just stared at each other like zombies. Jillian was the first to move, letting go of the steering wheel. Her shoulder muscles ached. Her left elbow throbbed. She didn't remember being thrown into the door, but knew she must have been.

"Megan?" Jillian's hands sank into her lap. "Are you okay?"

"I'm…I'm good." Megan's voice shook. "Did we…hit her?"

"No." Turning, Jillian gazed out through the windshield. The headlights barely reached the woman. Jillian gasped. She had expected to see the woman standing in the middle of the road, but she wasn't. She was sprawled on the pavement.

Jillian tried to take a deep breath but couldn't. She hadn't hit the woman. She was sure of it. And yet she must have.

She needed to call 911. She needed to get out of the

car. Needed to help the woman. Do whatever she could until an ambulance arrived.

Numbly, Jillian searched the center console. Finding her cell phone, she flipped it open.

"No service." Shoving the phone into her pocket, she was shocked to find that she was alone in the car. Megan had already climbed out. By the time Jillian caught up to her sister, Megan was already searching for a pulse.

"I can't feel anything!" Megan shifted her fingers to a new position on the woman's neck.

The woman was somewhere in her twenties—maybe even close to Megan's age. The blue business suit that the blond woman wore was ripped and filthy, and she was barefoot.

Whoever she was, she obviously wasn't a hiker or camper. So what in the hell had she been doing out here at this time of night? In a remote area. All alone and—

Alone?

Jillian stared down at the woman again, her gaze locking on the woman's wrists. The bruises circling them were dark and uniform. As was the discoloration around the ankles.

The dread and fear that had been pooling low in Jillian's body suddenly poured through her, reaching her lungs, forcing her breathing to go quick and shallow.

Jillian suddenly recalled how the woman had looked over her shoulder at the last moment. Was it possible that she hadn't been looking for a way to avoid being hit? That she'd been expecting to see something coming after her?

Or *someone?*

Jillian grabbed Megan by the upper arm. She tried

to pull her sister to her feet. "Come on. We need to get out of here. Now!"

Megan jerked free, but almost fell across the woman in the process, catching herself at the last minute. She looked up at Jillian. "Are you crazy? We can't leave her here like this!"

"I wasn't going to." Keeping an eye on the woods, Jillian grasped the woman's ankles.

"What are you doing?" Megan tried to break Jillian's hold. "You can't—"

"Get her arms." If she was still alive—and Jillian had her doubts—the woman's best chance was for them to load her into the car and get the hell out of here.

Assuming the convertible was still drivable. She'd been so focused on the woman that she hadn't given any thought to the condition of the car.

"But—"

Jillian straightened, hefting the weight of the woman's lower body. The blue skirt slid up, exposing more dried blood and bruising. Anger flashed through Jillian's veins. She'd seen photographs of injuries like this before, knew their cause.

"Get her damn arms, Megan!"

"Moving her might—"

"Look at those bruises… No car did that. She's been raped." Jillian glanced at the woods. "We need to get out of here now!"

Megan's fingers immediately closed around the woman's wrists, but it was still several seconds more before she actually got to her feet. They stood facing each other, the woman's dead weight slung between them. "We'll make it," Jillian said. Not because she believed it, but because she wanted Megan to. "Ready?"

With each awkward shuffle forward, they were forced to refine their hold as the woman's wrists and ankles turned slick with fresh blood. Dead bodies didn't bleed. Was it possible that the pressure she and Megan were exerting was causing the illusion of bleeding? Or was the woman actually still alive?

"We need…we need to pick up the pace here, Meg."

Megan nodded wordlessly. Her breathing was coming just as fast as Jillian's now. They were still twenty yards from the car when they both heard something and looked in the direction of the vehicle.

Backlit by headlights, the silhouette of a man came toward them. Not from the woods, but from where they'd left the car.

The sound of his boot heels striking the pavement echoed in the silence. Silence? She looked toward her car. Jillian had left the engine running. It no longer was.

Blood rushed in Jillian's ears, her heart slamming against her ribs. She heard the panicked, in-drawn breath of her sister and knew Megan shared her fear.

The man tossed Jillian's car keys into the air, and caught them easily. Then he started whistling a tune. She couldn't see the grin on his face, but she suspected it was there. Just as she suspected that his slow, easy swagger was born of his belief that instead of one possibly dead female, he now had two very live ones.

He was tall—six-two or -three—and appeared to be built solidly. Not the kind of man that even two women could easily overpower. He didn't seem to be carrying a weapon. But could she really bank on that?

"Megan?"

It wasn't until Jillian said her sister's name a second time that Megan finally pulled her gaze away from the man. But even as Jillian lowered the woman to the ground, Megan just watched.

"We can't do anything for her now, Meg." Jillian inched toward her sister.

"We can't leave her." Megan's voice was low. Strained.

"We have to." Jillian forcibly peeled Megan's fingers from around the woman's wrist.

Leaving the woman on the pavement, Jillian backed away, taking Megan with her. She would have expected the man to pick up his pace, but he didn't.

The pressure in her chest built. Jillian checked the road and then the trees on either side. Which way? Staying on the road wouldn't buy them any advantage. They hadn't passed any cars or seen any sign of civilization.

She checked the side of the road. The girl had come out of the trees to the right.

"The woods on the left," Jillian murmured as her fingers tightened around Megan's lower arm. "When I tell you, we're going to make a run for them."

Megan glanced over her shoulder, effectively giving away their escape route. Jillian couldn't worry about that just now. The whistling grew louder, the man closer. She felt her sister inch backward. Megan's shoulders straightened imperceptibly.

That she seemed to have pulled it together some encouraged Jillian. But would Megan be able to react fast enough when the time came? And what was Jillian going to do if her sister didn't? How was she going to protect Megan?

Remembering the cell phone in her pocket, needing the assurance that it was still there, Jillian slipped her hand inside.

The whistling stopped. As she watched, the man reached back and grabbed a shotgun that must have been strapped to his back. He brought it down and into position in a single, fluid motion.

"Get your hands where I can see them."

She'd already started to obey his command when the sudden blast of the sawed-off shotgun sent a dozen ricocheting pellets into Jillian's left shin, the pain like that of matches being shoved into her flesh.

"Make one more move, and the next one will cut you both in two."

He had reached the downed woman, but simply stepped over her as if she were some animal.

Jillian hobbled in place. Even if they made it to the woods, there was no guarantee of escape. They couldn't outrun a shotgun.

But what other choice did they have?

"Meg?" Jillian kept her voice low. She tightened her hold on her sister's arm until she felt her wince. "Nothing has changed. Even with the gun. Our best chance is to make a run for it. You understand?"

Megan offered a solemn nod.

The man was close enough now that Jillian could see his face. His lips curved upward as he focused on Megan, as if he found her fear amusing.

When the man's gaze returned to her, Jillian shifted slightly in front of Megan. For some reason, with his next step, he lowered the weapon to his side.

Jillian didn't hesitate. "Now!"

As Megan turned to run, Jillian rushed their attacker. As she closed the distance, her vision tunneled down until all she could see was the end of the shotgun barrel as it came up again.

The twin barrels appeared overlarge, like two soulless eyes summoned to witness her death. She'd had a rough start in life, and it looked as if the ending wasn't going to be much different. But all she could think about was the years that had stretched between. The sister who even now was escaping. She had always wondered how she could repay the Sorensens for everything they had given her.

Now she knew.

A shotgun blast exploded, the sound nearly taking Jillian to her knees. It took her several seconds to realize that she hadn't been hit. That the gun the man held hadn't gone off.

Megan!

Comprehension dawning slowly, she lifted her chin and stared at the man in front of her.

He smiled as a third explosion chewed the night.

"No!" Jillian whirled toward the trees on the left—the trees where Megan had disappeared.

As she leaped toward them, the man drove the gunstock into the back of her skull.

Chapter Two

The pain started at the back of Jillian's head but radiated throughout her body. The floor under her vibrated and swayed. Cold. She was so damned cold. And there was a strong odor of urine in her nostrils. Like a public restroom.

A sour taste filled her mouth. Vomit? Had she gotten drunk? Was that why her head hurt and everything seemed to be moving?

Fighting a surge of nausea, she forced open her eyes and faced total darkness, the kind that had frightened her as a child and at the moment still did.

Where was she? She tried to lift her head, to get her bearings, but nearly passed out as agony radiated through her skull.

Don't move. She sucked in a shallow breath. Then another. *That's it.* Just breathe.

In the process of trying to round up enough saliva to swallow, Jillian realized the vile taste came from some type of pill caught between her lip and her lower front teeth. She spit it out, but, as another wave of pain overtook her, wondered if she'd made a mistake. Maybe it had been an aspirin.

Jillian tried again to clear her head. Had she hit it somehow? Fallen? But why would she be lying in straw that reeked of urine? In what seemed to be some sort of moving vehicle? Some type of truck?

From the way that sound bounced around the space, it seemed to be a fairly large one.

Moving carefully this time, she shifted, looking for a more comfortable position. Her arms felt heavy, weighted down. She shifted her legs but recoiled when her left shin touched the straw. It felt as if someone had stabbed her there repeatedly with an ice pick. And it wasn't just her shin and head that hurt, either. Her whole body ached.

What in the hell had happened to her? Had she been in some kind of accident?

A gun blast…

Everything came back to her in a horrible rush. She and Megan had been driving down to Charleston. The woman in the road. The man with the shotgun.

Jillian clenched her eyes as the next memory hunted her down there in the dark. The sound of a shot fired in the woods. Dread filled her chest. Megan. She searched her memory but couldn't recall what happened next.

"Megan?" In her head, she screamed her sister's name, but she knew in reality her voice had barely been a whisper.

"Jill—Jilly? That…that you?" Megan's voice came from right behind her.

Ignoring the pain, Jillian reached out. A chain rattled and she realized there truly was weight around her wrist. A single manacle. She was chained up.

"Jilly? Where are you?"

"Here." Unable to see, she scooted toward her sister's voice. Was there enough slack in the chain to reach her?

To her surprise, she found her sister lying almost next to her in the straw. Fumbling her way upward along Megan's arms, Jillian discovered that her sister was chained up, too. Jillian ran her fingers up until she found Megan's face. Her cheeks were cool to the touch. "Megan? Are you okay? I heard a gunshot. Were you hit?"

"N-no." Her sister's voice sounded slurred. "They…they gave me some kind of pill. You, too."

Turning away, Jillian forced a finger down her own throat. She immediately retched into the straw, but it took several more attempts before she actually vomited. And it wasn't until she dry heaved that Jillian finally sank back to the floor. How much of the drug had already reached her system, though?

Suddenly recalling her cell phone, Jillian dug into her jacket pockets but didn't find it. No doubt they'd taken it from her.

"Megan?" When her sister didn't respond, she nudged her. "I need you to force a finger down your throat."

"Tried. Did….didn't work."

Jillian shook Megan's shoulder hard. "I need you to try again."

Megan obediently turned onto her side.

As Jillian listened to her sister's repeated attempts to vomit, she wondered about the woman they'd tried to save. Had she made it? Or was she already dead? And if dead, had they left her in the middle of the road? Or was she concealed somewhere close by in the dark?

She recalled their attacker's confidence. He'd seemed unconcerned about discovery.

"No…good," Megan said after long moments. "This is all my fault…getting us lost."

"Neither of us is responsible." Jill moved closer, straining to see. Megan appeared to be lying on her side, her knees drawn to her chest.

Jillian smoothed the hair back from Megan's forehead. "Tell me everything you can. How many are there?"

"Two."

"Was I out very long?"

"Don't…don't know," Megan mumbled. "Tired. Cold."

"What about the woman? Do you know what they did with her?"

"Here."

Jillian scanned the intense darkness. "Lady. Are you there?" she called, and then waited for any sign of life. When there was none, she leaned over her sister again. "Did the men say anything?"

Megan pulled her legs even tighter to her chest. "Say 'bout what?"

Jillian gave her sister a gentle shake. "Where they're taking us. What they plan to do with us."

She didn't really expect her sister to know those answers. Obviously, Megan was half-gone with whatever they'd given her.

"Kill…us. Like woman."

"They said that?" Jillian waited for her sister to

answer, but she didn't. "Megan?" Jillian gave her a hard shake this time. "Stay with me."

But when she still didn't respond, Jillian sat back. With Megan out, it was going to be up to Jillian to protect both of them. But how? As long as they were chained up, they were pretty much helpless.

Jillian propped her back against the mesh wall and carefully straightened her injured leg. If she flexed her toes, she could just reach the opposite mesh wall. If she had to make a guess, the truck must normally be used to haul some type of livestock.

Given the truck's speed, she assumed the road they were on to be a secondary one and not a major highway. Was it possible that she'd been unconscious only a short time? That they hadn't gone all that far? Were still in the Francis Marion National Forest?

If she could get them free from the shackles and get the back doors open, they could wait for the truck to slow even more and…

Jillian tried forcing the manacle over her hand. Unsuccessful, she collapsed her palm at the same time as she pulled. Continuing to manipulate the cuff, she rocked it back and forth as she twisted.

She added some hard-to-come-by spit to her wrist. She'd been fortunate to avoid the full dose of whatever they'd given Megan, but she couldn't count on that happening a second time. Once drugged, there would be no hope of escape.

Just as there was already no hope of rescue.

With no witnesses to their abduction, who would miss them? No one back home expected to hear from them. And even though they had confirmed reservations at one of Charleston's better hotels, the hotel staff wasn't likely to call the authorities when Jillian and Megan failed to check in. They'd run the cost for one night's stay through on Jillian's credit card and then cancel the other two nights. And when Jillian didn't show up for her job interview tomorrow, her résumé would hit the circular file. End of story.

Eventually someone might find Jillian's abandoned car. But by the time the police were brought in, the trail would be cold. The story of two missing sisters might make *America's Most Wanted,* but after a few months another kidnapping, another unfortunate incident would push their plight into the background. And with no family to stoke anyone's memory, she and Megan would be forgotten.

She couldn't let that happen. It couldn't end like this. She wouldn't allow it. Somehow. Some way. They were going to survive this.

In sudden frustration, Jillian tore at the manacle and in the process peeled open the heel of her hand. Cursing, fighting tears, she bent over her wrist. She'd heard of animals chewing off a paw to escape a trap and of people cutting off a limb just to survive, but she didn't have any type of instrument to accomplish an amputation. And even if she did, she doubted that she could actually go through with the self-mutilation. At least not yet.

But would it come to that? Would there come a time when she'd be willing to do just about anything? She decided it might be best not to think about the future. Swallowing her tears, Jillian ran her hands upward over the wire-mesh wall to the overhead mesh. For now she needed a skinny piece of metal.

She'd only picked one lock in her life and there'd been someone standing over her shoulder the whole time, explaining the process, but at least it would keep her from going crazy while she came up with something better.

With a quick indrawn breath, she jerked her fingers back, having encountered something sharp. After several seconds, going back to the same spot, she explored more cautiously but just as desperately.

A sharp scraping sound, like nails across a chalkboard, shrieked from overhead. Even though she was encased in suffocating blackness, Jillian stopped moving and stared upward for several seconds. When another screech followed the first, she realized it was just a low tree limb dragging across the outside of the truck, and went back to what she was doing.

It seemed as if she'd exhausted every inch of available surface before she finally located a piece of metal that wasn't firmly attached on one end. With her second attempt to break it off, she managed to rip off the meaty end of her finger instead. With the sixth attempt, she jammed it beneath her fingernail. With no other choice, and blood now interfering with her ability to grasp, she continued as best she could, stopping only when she could no longer hold her arm above her head.

Finally the two-inch length of metal broke free and immediately fell into the straw.

Desperately, Jillian foraged. This was literally a needle in a haystack. She'd never find it. Panic tightened her chest, as dread deepened inside her. As long as she had a course of action, she'd been okay, but suddenly the ability to cope evaporated.

After several difficult seconds, she managed to partially rein in the panic. She needed to keep it together. The piece of metal would be heavier than the straw. Maybe it had dropped through the bedding, was resting against the floor. Finding the piece of metal where the back wall met the floor, Jillian picked it up and settled back, her manacled hand resting in her lap.

Holding the crude pick between the thumb and first two fingers of her free hand, she used the remaining two fingers to locate the lock, then in an awkward movement attempted to shift the pick forward and into the opening. She kept at it even after her fingers had gone numb from the pain and the cold.

The truck slowed to make a sweeping right turn. Everything seeming to creak and shift at once—the metal overhead, the wood wall next to Megan, the floorboards under Jillian. Holding her breath, Jillian waited for the truck to accelerate. When it finally did, it wasn't nearly as fast. Were they stopping?

Frantic, she shifted into a different position and jammed the metal pick down. The lock suddenly clicked, and the manacle slid off with a soft clang.

Jillian immediately rolled onto her knees. As she reached for Megan's handcuff, her sister stirred.

"Megan, wake up!"

"Jilly?"

"I'm free," Jillian said. "We just need to get you loose, too."

Megan tried to sit up, but quickly lost her balance and flopped into the straw again. When she tried to sit up the next time, Jillian stopped her. "It might be better if you don't try to help me."

"Hurry."

Jillian had expected it to be easier the second time, but quickly realized that her first success had been nothing more than sheer luck. She jabbed the piece of metal into the opening.

Suddenly braking again, the truck made a hard left and immediately adopted a waddling motion as if it rode the ruts of a washed-out road.

Losing her balance, Jillian wobbled forward, then was thrown backward, her right shoulder and the side of her head bouncing off the mesh. Brake pads squealed as the truck slowed; its tires churned through soft sand or mud for a minute or more before giving up.

As soon as the truck came to a halt, Jillian reached for Megan's wrist again.

"Why did they stop?" Megan mumbled.

Jillian listened as she worked at the lock, asking herself the same question. Was the stop only temporary? Had they stopped to relieve themselves? To check their route?

Two seconds later the engine was shut down. In the ensuing silence, the sound of the radio in the cab drifted through, the station a country-western one.

A door opened, the hinges screeching for oil. Jillian briefly heard the rumble of male conversation. She went still, waiting to find out if a second door would be opened.

Her brain leapfrogged. What was she going to do? And how? And when? She'd been so focused on getting free of the manacle, seeing that as the first obstacle, that she hadn't given any thought to the next step.

Jillian searched for the handcuff that she'd removed only minutes earlier. Finding it, she pulled it next to her. Did she have the courage to place it around her wrist again?

When the cab door suddenly slammed, Megan and Jillian both jerked. Jillian immediately rotated Megan's cuff until she found the lock, but neither woman spoke.

Nearly a minute later, there came a rhythmic sound that Jillian couldn't identify. What did it matter, anyway, what they were doing? What was important was getting Megan free.

What about the woman from the road, though? What if she was still alive? If she was chained up, too, which Jillian assumed she would be, there wasn't time to free her.

But how could they leave her behind?

Having ceased for nearly a minute, the sound started up again, outside. Megan shifted. "Oh God...they're digging. Why?"

Jillian tried to ignore the question. The answer was too obvious.

"Jilly?"

"Don't think about it." But now that Jillian knew the origin of the sound, she could no longer block it out. Was that the reason they'd stopped? Was the woman dead and they intended to bury her?

Or were they digging three graves?

The sound stopped. The silence that followed was even more frightening.

When the latch on the truck's rear door rattled, Megan pushed Jillian away. "No more time."

"I'm not going without you."

"One of us gets away, the other...better chance." Megan's fingers, suddenly strong, grabbed Jillian's arm. "Go! Get help."

The sound of the door being shoved upward was like that of a small roller coaster clattering to a stop. As moonlight penetrated the interior, Jillian got a look at their surroundings.

At first, she thought she'd hallucinated. That the drugs were somehow responsible for what she was seeing. But as Megan stiffened beside her, she knew that she wasn't that lucky.

Oh God!

There had to be at least six young women—maybe even teenagers—out cold and chained up like livestock, one to a mesh stall. Some wore only shorts and T-shirt. Others had on jeans and sweaters. Despite the cool temperature in the truck, there were no blankets covering any of them.

The woman they'd been trying to save was there, too. Her light-blue skirt wrapped her waist like a thick belt, and her blouse lay open, exposing her rib cage. She wasn't in a stall, though, and didn't appear to be restrained like the rest. Did that mean she was dead?

As a man climbed up into the truck, his body briefly blocked the moonlight. It wasn't the same gun-toting scum from the road. This one was closer to Jillian's height, five-seven or five-eight, and was dressed in jeans and cowboy boots.

As if he had a single objective, he headed to the front of the truck. Once there, he nudged the woman from the road. When she didn't respond, he dug the toe of his boot into her back and gave a hard shove, rolling her without resistance onto her belly.

Next, he grabbed her by the arms and hauled her to a spot just inside the door. As he returned to the front of the cargo area again, he pulled a medicine bottle from a front pocket and shook out a pill, clearly intending to dose the other women.

Already unconscious, the first one didn't fight when he shoved whatever it was into her mouth. He moved counterclockwise to the next girl. She wore jeans, a pink sweatshirt and a pair of athletic shoes. "Come on, darlin'. You know the routine."

. He used her hair to roughly pull her head around, and then pried open her mouth. She appeared younger than the others, or maybe she was just smaller.

Jillian watched through slitted eyes. How often did they drug them? Every four hours? More often? Less often? Would she and Megan have more drugs forced into their mouths in the next few minutes, or would he skip them this time?

As he moved on to the next, Jillian glanced at Megan. But with eyes filled with shock, Megan stared at the woman from the road. Jillian wanted to reach out to Megan and offer comfort, but couldn't because she needed to keep the empty manacle concealed. Maybe if they were lucky, he wouldn't stop to check on them. Obviously, they hadn't reached their final destination. The only reason they'd stopped was to bury the woman. Given more time, Jillian could free Megan.

But even once they were free, there would be the problem of getting out of the truck, since the back door was locked on the outside.

She'd made her decision by the time he stepped in front of her. If he didn't notice that she was free, she'd stay put. If he did…

When he nudged her with his boot as he had the

woman from the road, she grunted softly as if too out of it to do any more.

But then he reached down and pulled on the chain; the empty manacle swung free. "What the…?"

Jillian kicked hard. He avoided the blow. But not the one Megan landed against the back of his knee.

"Bitch!" He tried to grab the mesh wall for support, but instead went down hard.

Even as Jillian snapped the manacle around his wrist and vaulted over him, he was already yelling for his partner.

Jillian hesitated just inside the door, looking out at the dark surrounding trees, looking out at freedom. But she couldn't jump. It was as if she were still shackled in place.

"Go!" Megan screamed.

The second man climbed out of the cab. Though she couldn't see him, she heard the sound of a shotgun round being chambered.

"Now," Megan shouted as she kicked at Jillian's ankle. "You have to go now."

Her muscles frozen, Jillian turned back to her sister. "I'll be back for you. No matter what."

In the split second before the second man came into view, Jillian did the most difficult thing she'd ever done in her life.

She jumped.

Chapter Three

Jillian raced for the trees. Rain pummeled down. She plunged into the woods as a shotgun exploded behind her, leaves shredding less than a foot away. A second round quickly followed. Without looking back she careened forward, dodging trees, her feet slipping on wet leaves, her hands out in front warding off small branches.

There was not time to think about what she'd just done, about the sister she'd left behind. There was survival.

Seconds later she heard the men crashing after her, one following in her wake, the other off to the right, as if trying to block access to the road.

A wasted effort. If the area was remote enough that they hadn't hesitated to use a shotgun, even if she reached the road, she was unlikely to find immediate help—the only kind that was going to do her or Megan any good.

For now she'd stick to the woods, hope to either lose or outrun them. But where was she? How far from where they'd been kidnapped?

She fell several times, but came up like a sprinter out

of a starting blocks, attacking the gauntlet of oaks and pines and the leaf-covered stumps. She was gasping for air now, her lungs aching. How much longer could she continue the grueling pace? How much farther could she go?

Blocking out those thoughts, she substituted others. *Keep moving. Stay ahead of them. Don't look back.*

There finally came a point when she couldn't do any of those things, though, and like an animal run to ground, she collapsed.

Fear spiked through Jillian as she lay heaving, the rain slashing through the tree canopy, reaching her, splattering her chilled skin. Minutes crept by as she listened, as she prayed, and as she considered what she was going to do if she actually had outrun them. She couldn't waste time stumbling around these woods, hoping to find a house.

Which left only one option—the road. Jillian stumbled to her feet, stood there unsteadily, briefly staring back the way she'd come. Once satisfied that she wasn't being watched, she turned and headed in what she hoped was the direction of the road.

But even when she reached the narrow and unlined pavement, she remained hidden in the bordering trees, recalling how the woman she and Megan had tried to save had exploded from similar woods.

The kidnappers weren't dumb. They'd know that sooner or later she'd have to make for the road.

Was that how they'd caught the other woman? By waiting for her to go for it?

Jillian's fear was so strong that even when she saw the headlights of an oncoming car, she found it difficult to get to her feet.

What if it was a trap? What if instead of being rescued, of helping to save Megan, Jillian was about to be captured again?

Realizing that there was no other choice, Jillian raced onto the road and into the path of an oncoming car.

Tuesday, 2:18 a.m.

RICK BRADY AWAKENED abruptly, momentarily disoriented. As the phone rang a second time, he rolled toward it, squinting at the clock as he went.

It was after two in the morning. Who would be calling?

When he'd been with Charleston PD, it wasn't unusual to be called out in the middle of the night sometimes. And because he had, back then, he'd slept where he could easily reach the phone. But he'd been a civilian for nearly five years now, long enough for the habit to die.

He was still attempting to free himself from the sheets when it rang a third time, and he suddenly encountered something warm and solid stretched out next to him.

"Move it, Bax," Rick mumbled.

The eleven-year-old male golden retriever that had been sleeping with its head on the second pillow grumbled, but didn't get out of the way until forced off the bed. As soon as his paws hit the wood floor, though, Bax was on the move, bounding back onto the mattress and heading for the warm spot vacated by Rick.

Having finally located the phone among the pile of law magazines, Rick took a few more seconds to clear his head. He ran a hand over his face and squinted at the caller ID.

"PRIVATE."

The phone rang a fourth time. He hit the talk button. "Rick Brady."

"Detective Nate Langley with the Charleston County Sheriff's Office."

The name wasn't one Rick recalled from his years on the force.

Propped against the headboard now, he did a quick mental scan of his current client list but came up empty. Not because those that he represented were incapable of murder, but because most of them were already behind bars for that particular felony. That was the up side of handling death-penalty appeals. Rick always knew where to find his clients. Unless…

Had one of them escaped?

"I know it's late," Langley said.

"What can I do for you, Detective? I assume this has something to do with one of my clients."

There was a pause. "No. I'm actually looking for some help with a case."

Rick remained silent, waiting for the detective to go on.

It took several seconds for Langley to take the hint. "Eight years ago your father was the lead detective on a case. The Midnight Run Murders."

"Go on."

"Is it true that even after his retirement, he continued to investigate? And that since his death, you've been doing the same?"

"Where is this conversation headed?" Rick abruptly swung his legs over the side of the bed and dragged the sheet across his lap. "And why call me at—" he eyed the clock "—two in the morning to ask?"

"There's been another incident."

Incident? It was an odd word choice. Especially when used in the same conversation with the Midnight Run Murders. His father had been obsessed with the case.

"And you think there's a connection?" It had been over six years since the official investigation of the Midnight Run Murders had ground to a halt and the case had gone cold for everyone but his father.

"I wouldn't be calling you if I didn't think there was a connection."

Hearing the irritation in Langley's voice, Rick found it more difficult to hold on to his own. "Any survivors?"

"One. She managed to escape. The rest appear to be headed south."

A witness? The last time there had been one, too. Unfortunately, she hadn't lived long enough to tell the cops anything.

Rick crossed to where he'd left his jeans hanging over a chair back. "Can she talk?" Holding the phone between his ear and his shoulder, he kicked his way into his jeans.

"Yes."

"Did she get a look at her kidnapper?"

"Make that plural, and yes."

There was a slamming sound on the other end of the line, like a car door being closed. Then the sounds of shouting in the background, of wind briefly hitting Langley's cell. "Hold on." The cell's receiver was momentarily covered as if Langley talked to someone, then he was back on the line. "Are you still there?"

"When did it happen?" Rick fastened his jeans.

"Around midnight. Listen, Brady. I don't usually

contact civilians, but given your background…" He paused for several seconds, as if uncomfortable with what he was about to say. "Right now I'll take help from anywhere I can get it."

"What kind are you looking for?"

"I'd like to get copies of everything you have. Any notes your father produced after he left the department. Anything you've turned up since your father's death."

He rarely discussed his interest in one of Charleston's most notorious murders—mostly because he believed that it was that same interest that had gotten his father killed. And while Rick wanted to find those responsible for his father's murder, he wanted to live long enough to do something about it.

"I can send a patrol officer by to get them," Langley offered.

If there hadn't been lives on the line, Rick might have refused Langley's request. For more than twenty-five years, Rick's father had been a cop with the Charleston County Sheriff's Office. When he'd needed his fellow officers the most, they'd let him down. Men he'd worked side by side with hadn't hesitated to accept that Jim Brady, suffering from cancer, had put a gun to his head and pulled the trigger.

Rick knew better. Jim Brady had never been a quitter. For nearly sixteen months Rick had been trying to get the investigation reopened.

Maybe now someone would be willing to listen to him.

Rick grabbed the sweatshirt from the chair back. "Don't bother sending anyone by. Where do you want me to deliver them?"

"The station."

Tuesday, 2:42 a.m.

AFTER HANGING UP with Langley, Rick had reconsidered what he'd just agreed to and decided the deal was too one-sided. Langley got copies of nearly eight years of investigation notes while giving up nothing in return. The way Rick figured it, a little reciprocity was in order.

Which was why he'd decided to drive out to the scene and deliver the records directly to Langley. Even if that hadn't been the case, though, once he'd made a call to one of his contacts at the sheriff's, and learned where the crime had occurred, there was no keeping him away.

As Rick's SUV coasted to a stop behind a line of police vehicles, he saw the rack lights of a single patrol car strobe through the trees off to the left.

Two black-and-whites passed him going fifty or sixty, heading north, their lights flashing, their tires turning the moisture on the road into a fine mist that trailed behind. There was no traffic at this time of night, which wasn't surprising since this narrow secondary road saw limited use even during daylight hours.

Most of the properties out this way were relics of the pre–Civil War South, plantations that had once been capable of supporting their owners. The reverse was true now. It was the owners who supported these white elephants. Or didn't. Many of the properties were vacant, their titles held by corporations, land speculators who gambled that when the last of South Carolina's coastline was built up, developers would look inland.

As soon as Rick climbed out of the sedan, a heavy wind gust forced his sweatshirt against his chest. The storm that had been sitting stationary out in the Atlantic for days had suddenly decided to make its move.

Closing the car door, Rick aimed the flashlight at a historic marker across the road. Ravenel Cemetery. His father's body had been found less than a quarter of a mile from where he now stood. Rick didn't believe in that kind of coincidence.

The Midnight Run Murders had haunted Rick's father. Just as his murder now haunted Rick. What had brought Jim Brady out here the last night of his life? Had he been following some new lead, or had he been lured out to this remote area? Rick knew he'd never be able to answer that question with any certainty. Just as he knew that no matter how much time passed, he would continue to hunt his father's killer.

Turning, he walked up the line of cars, crossing in front of the first in the group, a marked cruiser. Crime-scene tape had been wrapped around a century oak next to the dirt drive and then strung across to what was left of a stone pillar. The loose ends whipped in the breeze, as did the branches overhead.

The rookie officer handling the scene log had been staring back into the trees—probably feeling like the lone kid who hadn't been invited to the party—but when Rick approached, the officer moved to meet him. "This is an official scene."

From the phone call he'd made to a buddy of his at the sheriff's office Rick gathered that Langley was a by-the-rule type of cop. Which meant that selling him on the idea that Rick could be a valuable asset to the investigation was going to be tough if not impossible. But that's what he was going to have to do if he wanted any kind of toehold on the investigation.

But even if Rick wasn't able to sell Langley on the idea, at the very least he wanted a look at the scene. Which in turn might fuel a new direction for Rick's own investigation.

"I'm aware that it's a crime scene." Knowing the routine, Rick passed his driver's license. "Detective Langley contacted me. He's in need of some files that I have in my possession."

Everyone who showed up at a scene, every officer, every assistant district attorney, every medical examiner went through the same routine.

The officer checked the license, and then swung the flashlight up to Rick's face to make the comparison. Rick flipped off the baseball cap to make it easier.

"You can put the hat back on, sir." He lifted the radio to his mouth. "I have Rick Brady out here. Says he has some files for Detective Langley."

Nearly half a minute went by before there was a response. "This is Langley. Have Brady give you the files. Tell him I appreciate that he drove all the way out here to deliver them, but that I'm a little busy right now."

The officer lowered the radio. "I guess you heard?"

"Tell Langley I want a face-to-face before I turn over anything. And remind him that he's the one who called me in the middle of the night." Rick felt fairly certain that Langley wouldn't turn him down.

Rick was also hoping that Langley was busy, too busy to leave the scene. The last thing Rick wanted was for Langley to hike out for the meeting.

The rookie relayed the message.

"Send him down," Langley barked.

The rookie lowered the radio again and passed back Rick's ID. "Don't walk on the drive. Keep to the right of it. Clearing's a good thirty-five yards back in there." He lifted the yellow tape. "And I wouldn't expect much in the way of a welcome when you reach it."

Rick gave a curt nod before ducking under the barrier. The leaf mulch covering the soft ground made the going slick, and with each gust, the surrounding trees shed water from their leaves. He nearly lost his footing on a slight incline. He hated this time of year. The mud and the muck. The wet, gray days. The upcoming holidays where the families of his clients contacted him with tearful pleas.

The rack lights of the car in the clearing were suddenly shut down. It was only then that he noticed the flashlight beams deep in the woods off to his right.

For the past six months Rick's investigation of his father's murder had been limited almost exclusively to reexamining previous leads. Police work was like that sometimes, an old lead suddenly providing a new one. But even those had dried up. Tonight might possibly change that. What had taken place in these woods could bring new leads. New hope for finding his father's killer. And more misery, too, for the latest victims.

Rick had gone only a short distance when he spotted the tarp spread across an area of the drive. He assumed that it protected tire impressions that the scene techs hadn't gotten around to casting. If the officer hadn't been watching, Rick would have taken a quick look beneath it. As it was, he kept moving, unwilling to risk eviction for evidence tampering.

After another twenty feet, though, he stopped and looked back toward the main road. The lane curved just enough that the entrance was no longer visible. Nor was the officer.

Rick shone the flashlight beam onto the drive. It appeared as if two vehicles had used the entrance. One set of tracks belonged to the police vehicle. The other was made by some type of truck as it entered and then exited. The dual tires and larger wheel base were right for a delivery type.

He scanned a broader area with the flashlight, taking in both sides of the drive. A few small limbs were scattered about, torn from the tree by the weather or the passing truck. Either way the truck would have to have been on the small side not to do more damage to the low-hanging limbs.

All in all, the vehicle's size, the dual tires and larger wheel base were right for a delivery type, the kind that had been found at the scene eight years ago.

Rick squatted for a closer look. The tire impressions were still well defined. The tight tree canopy might act as a buffer against a hard downpour, but even if that were the case, the tracks still couldn't have been there long. Two or three hours at most. Two hours didn't sound like much time, but in an abduction case it was.

Up until that moment, he'd managed mostly to avoid thoughts about the current victims—because they were faceless, and because he'd been so callously focused on his own agenda. But as Rick got back to his feet, those faces began to take on the features of the previous victims.

He hadn't been assigned to the initial investigation eight years ago, hadn't been on the scene when the truck had been opened up for the first time, but he'd seen the photos. He'd seen the faces of the dead women. Five days of heat hadn't been enough time to dehumanize them.

But it had been long enough to make them unforgettable. Particularly to his father.

Just as Rick reached the clearing, another rain band roared through, the sound deafening. It came at him horizontally, forcing him to turn his back to catch his breath. It continued to pummel his shoulders and blast his bare neck with a knifelike intensity. He waited seconds, and then impatiently faced the deluge again.

The taillights of the patrol car that had been driven in—probably by the first officer to arrive—were a red blur now. Holding on to his ball cap, Rick cut toward the car, figuring Langley would have sought refuge there. No one would be crazy enough to stand out in this when there was shelter.

It wasn't until he got closer that he saw that there was no one in the car and that the headlights were aimed at a second tarp, this one spread out over a slightly raised area of ground. A crude grave? Or something else?

There had been no attempt to conceal the victims the last time, so if it was a grave, it meant a change in M.O. Or the possibility that the cases weren't connected. That he'd climbed out of a warm bed for nothing.

And as far as crime scenes went, it was unlikely to produce much in the way of usable evidence. The clearing was mostly deep grass, a few saplings, some crude building rubble left from some sort of structure that had long ago disintegrated. Even if the kidnappers had left anything behind, the rain had most likely taken care of it.

As quickly as it had started, the rain tapered to a

drizzle. A generator cranked up almost immediately, replacing the sound of nature's fury with one that was manmade. Portable floodlights snapped back to life.

As soon as they did, Rick spotted the man on the opposite side of the clearing. Because he was the only officer in the vicinity who didn't seem to be actively searching the ground for evidence, Rick felt fairly certain that he'd found Nate Langley. He was average height, five-nine or so, and wore a yellow slicker. Rick took in the man's clean-shaven head, undecided if it was an effort to disguise a receding hairline or an attempt to appear tougher.

A dark-haired woman, soaked with rain and hunched beneath a heavy blanket, stood next to the man. Rick frowned. If she was their witness, the one who got away, she was too old to fit the previous profile. The victims eight years ago had been much younger—fifteen to seventeen.

At Rick's approach, both glanced in his direction. The man said something to the woman, and she immediately turned and moved away as if wanting to avoid Rick.

But then again, maybe it had nothing to do with him. Perhaps she just wanted to escape contact with another stranger. To avoid yet another set of eyes watching her with speculation.

So why had she been allowed to remain? Why hadn't she been transported out of here?

Though she didn't go very far, she didn't look at Rick again. Instead she stared straight ahead, almost defiantly.

What had she seen tonight?

In spite of her condition—the wet hair, the muddy

clothes—she was striking. As she lifted the blanket, using it to wipe the rain from her face, her chin quivered and her hold on the blanket seemed to intensify.

Watching her, he recalled what it had been like to be called out in the middle of the night to preside over tragedy. This was the part of police work he was thankful to have left behind.

These days, by the time he became involved with perpetrators or victims, most of the heartache, the fear, was carefully concealed behind pride or belligerence. The insight left him unsettled.

The man moved to meet Rick. There was nothing welcoming in his face or in the extended hand, just the required professional greeting.

"Detective Langley." Langley's hand dropped. "I assume you have something for me. Besides the notes. Something that you felt compelled you to drive all the way out here to deliver personally."

"Actually, I thought you might have some questions for me. We both know that a favorable outcome is only possible if you move fast. You don't have time to wade through years of reports."

Langley cocked his head as he jabbed his hands into the pockets of the slicker. "I won't need to. At least not tonight. Kenny Lennox is on his way out here. You may recall that he worked the original investigation, right alongside your father."

"And the case went cold two years later. What Kenny had, what you'll be using in the next few hours to make crucial decisions, is two years' worth of investigation notes, of interviews that led nowhere. The information I have is much more current—"

"But no more conclusive. If it was, I wouldn't have needed to call you tonight, would I?"

Even though Langley looked ready to throw Rick out, Rick wasn't giving up.

He had positioned himself so that he could watch the woman over Langley's shoulder. Langley hadn't even been living in Charleston when the previous murders had taken place. Was it possible that he just hadn't asked the right questions? That she knew more than she'd already revealed?

He refocused on Langley. "My father believed that there was a Charleston connection. Kenny Lennox didn't. Last theory I heard out of Kenny's mouth was the kidnappers were just passing through."

The woman suddenly took several steps toward where two crime-scene techs spread a second tarp next to the first. Rick knew what was about to happen—if there was a body beneath that pile of dirt, it was going to be dug up.

Did the woman know who was in the grave, then?

When Rick glanced at Langley, he realized the detective was also watching her. As his gaze reconnected with Rick's, Langley's face tightened. "I appreciate your bringing out the records and your offer to help, but my men can take it from here."

"You do realize that the Midnight Run victims were younger than your witness over there? They were all in their late teens."

Even as he said it, Rick was thinking about an officer who had just walked out of the woods thirty or so feet to the east of them. Langley had his men still searching the woods. Why? What were they looking for? More victims that were still alive? Or more graves?

"I'm aware that the previous victims were in their late teens. And that the crime scene eight years ago was less than a mile from here. And that the spot where your father was found was even less than that." He wiped at his face. "This is an official investigation. I don't need you mucking this up to further your own agenda."

Langley waved over the officer Rick had noticed seconds earlier. "I'll have one of my men accompany you back to your car to collect those files. I'll have them copied and get the originals back to you by morning."

Langley's cell phone rang. As he checked the caller ID, the lead detective moved away, turning his back in dismissal before actually answering.

The officer Langley had motioned over continued toward them. There was no way Rick was leaving now. When he arrived, Rick held out his car keys. "It's the silver Explorer at the back of the line. The boxes I brought for Detective Langley are on the backseat."

The officer glanced toward his superior as if wanting some indication that this was why he'd been called over, but Langley's back was turned and he was still on the phone.

After several seconds more of obvious internal debate, the officer took the key ring. "Silver SUV, right?"

"Three boxes."

As soon as the officer walked away, Rick's gaze swung to the woman. She continued to stare at the tarp.

Was he really the kind of son of a bitch who would use the victim of a crime to further his own agenda?

As it turned out, he was.

Chapter Four

Finally.

Jillian watched the two crime-scene officers—one tall and lanky, the other much shorter—spread out a yellow tarp next to the blue one. Everywhere else in the clearing the wild grasses remained knee-high, but here in this fifteen-by-fifteen area it had been trampled into a tawny carpet. The still-covered mound sat dead center and in a low spot, surrounded by a shallow, ever-widening moat.

Even though the men were dressed for the muddy conditions in black rain gear and rubber boots, they still sank ankle deep with each step, and each attempt to pull free of the muck was accompanied by incessant sucking sounds. As much as she hated the rain and the mud, it had been the deep tire tracks left by the kidnappers' truck that had led them into these woods. Without them, the cops might still be looking for the right clearing.

Jillian struggled to drag the soaked blanket that slid

down her arms up to her shoulders again. With her knees threatening to go soft on her like those of a weightlifter struggling with a too-heavy barbell, she widened her stance for stability.

But no sooner had she dealt with that than her teeth started to chatter together. Jillian stiffened her jaw muscles to conceal it. She was dead on her feet, the last of her energy reserves depleted to the point her body was struggling to maintain its core temperature. She was familiar with the equation. Wet clothes and temperatures in the forties added up to hypothermia.

Which seemed mild compared to what her sister might be facing right now if…if she was still alive. As much as she wanted to believe that her sister wasn't dead, Jillian knew she had to be prepared for the worst. That it wouldn't be just the woman from the road who was buried ten feet from her, but Megan, too.

She had tried sitting in the patrol car, but hadn't been able to handle the confinement. Nor was she certain how much longer she'd be able to deal with the inactivity, the waiting. How long before she lost control? Until the screams that exploded silently behind her ribs finally escaped? Before she ripped aside the tarp and used her bare hands?

Her shoulders shook violently two or three times before she could control the shaking. Needing to look away, Jillian glanced over her shoulder to see what Langley was up to. He no longer stood next to the stranger, but was talking on his cell phone. Again. His back was to her, which suited her fine. She didn't like the detective much, and trusted him even less. From the moment he'd shown up, he'd refused to answer most of her questions. And the few answers he had provided were vague.

"What was being done to locate the truck?" "Everything."

"Had the FBI been notified?" "No, and they wouldn't be until the initial investigation was complete."

She'd heard bits and pieces of conversation between the other officers, enough to know that Detective Langley was lying through his teeth, or at the very least keeping something from her.

She eyed the newcomer. Unlike Langley, he hadn't moved away. The jeans and sweatshirt that he wore looked soaked, yet he didn't give any indication that he was particularly cold. In fact, he looked at ease, as if he were accustomed to what was happening.

She'd have sworn the man was a cop, but when she'd asked Langley about him as the man had approached them, the detective had bluntly ordered her to stay clear of him. Why? Because he was worried about what the stranger might reveal to her? Or because he was afraid of what Jillian might reveal to the stranger?

Either way, Jillian didn't like being ordered around and manipulated any more than she liked being lied to. If she hadn't been afraid that Langley would have her hauled to town for it—something he'd been threatening to do since he'd finished questioning her—she would have already approached the stranger.

As if he'd known he was being watched, the man suddenly glanced in her direction and caught her staring. Instead of looking away almost immediately as the other officers did, his gaze remained steady. Direct. She decided she liked that. For several seconds they simply regarded each other. Jillian was the first to look away.

The blanket began to slip again. She tightened her hold on it. Despite the amount of rain that she'd stood through, mud still caked her jeans all the way to the knees. A plastic shoe cover had replaced the shoe she'd lost during her escape, but it was cold enough now that her foot had gone nearly numb. Unfortunately, her left shin, the one that had been hit by the ricocheting shot, hadn't.

"Ma'am." The tall, lanky officer who had been handling the tarp walked toward her. The rain had plastered his dark hair to his pale scalp, and because of the short length and the thin texture, it resembled a skullcap. "We're going to need you to step back another few feet."

She offered a silent nod and shuffled backward as requested, watched as he returned to help the other crime-scene officer. This time when she tried to hike up the blanket, it got away from her and plunked to the ground. As she bent to retrieve it, the sudden pressure of tears forced her to straighten, leaving it in the mud. All in all she was a physical wreck and an emotional basket case.

Jillian picked a point in the woods to stare at, and, taking a deep breath, held it. She couldn't fall apart now.

Out of the corner of her eye she caught a flash of yellow.

"This will keep you from getting any wetter."

Though she hadn't heard the newcomer's approach, he was standing next to her, holding out a slicker, probably the same one she'd foolishly turned down when Langley had offered it nearly an hour ago.

This time she took it. "Thanks."

He was taller than she'd first thought. Or perhaps she

was just feeling so damn small that he seemed that way. He wore a light blue sweatshirt with Citadel monogrammed in nearly the same color thread, jeans, a baseball cap and muddy hiking boots.

The rain that trailed down the side of his neck was tinged blue from the ball cap, as was the water dripping off the end of his nose and running down his neck in rivulets. He needed a shave, or maybe he was just one of those men who thought a day-old, scratchy beard appealed to women.

She tried working the zipper, but her fingers were stiff.

"Let me do that."

She immediately twisted away slightly. "That's okay. I've got it." Why was it that she suddenly felt even more vulnerable? Was it just because in a matter of moments, she could be facing her worst nightmare? Surrounded by strangers?

She flinched when he gave the attached hood a light tug.

He lowered his hand. "You might want to use that, too."

Nodding, Jillian pulled it up, and then immediately slipped her hands into the pockets. Even closed, the coat offered little in the way of warmth, but at least it blocked some of the wind, and weighed less than the quilt.

"The name's Rick Brady."

"Jillian. Jillian Sorensen." She glanced toward Langley, who was still on the phone, then at Rick Brady again. "Are you a cop?"

"No. I used to be."

"So if you're not a cop, what are you doing here?"

"Detective Langley phoned."

"Why?" The question was more reflexive than probing.
. "Long story."

Intent on watching the two officers uncover the mound, Jillian let the matter drop. Her abdominal muscles tightened with dread. She tried not to envision what was to come, but she couldn't stop herself. Maybe because violence was nothing new to her. The first five years of her life had been filled with it, and with the unending fear that it brought.

Rick suddenly stepped out in front of her, his wide chest blocking her view. "There's no reason to go through this. My car's out on the road. We could wait there. I'm sure someone would—"

Shaking her head slowly, Jillian shoved her hands a little deeper into the pockets. She lifted her chin and met his gaze. "You don't understand. I need to be here. For Megan… For my sister…"

His gray eyes narrowed, and he looked as if he wanted to say something, but he didn't. Instead he slowly stepped aside, remaining close enough that his elbow brushed her slicker.

Jillian felt her breath catch as the first crime-scene officer forced his shovel into the dirt. Instead of tossing the contents onto the tarp, he placed it carefully. The second man did the same, and after several rotations a rhythm was established—as one man sliced open the earth, the other unloaded his shovel.

She tried to close off the sound, to not think about the terror-filled moments when she had listened to it earlier tonight.

The three officers assigned to search the tall grass in

the clearing had stopped what they were doing and now stood on the opposite side of the grave, watching their coworkers labor. Unlike Jillian's view of the deepening hole, theirs had remained unblocked by the growing pile of dirt. And unlike Jillian, no matter what the grave revealed, they would go home to their wives, their girl-friends, their lives.

Did they take life for granted the way she had?

Ducking her head and closing her eyes, Jillian crossed her arms in front of her and just listened. The sharp scrape of shovels collecting wet soil, the dull plop as it was discarded, the wind pulling at the trees, the close-by movements of feet through the tall grass.

And then it wasn't distant sounds that she heard, but those closer by. The sound of Rick shifting next to her. She realized that even with the scene unfolding before them, she was continually aware of him standing beside her. She found his presence, the presence of this stranger, oddly comforting. Feeling her body sway toward him, she opened her eyes, focusing on the action in front of her.

The tall, lanky digger paused with shovel in hand.

Her heart hammered behind her ribs. The muscles of her chest tightened. Tears that she had been keeping under control began to build again. *Breathe.* She had to keep breathing. She had to keep it together.

As the shorter man climbed to his feet again, the other one left his shovel anchored upright in the ground and carefully stepped around the pile of dirt. "Detective Langley?"

Langley was still on the phone, but hung up imme-diately and strode toward the grave. Detouring, he stopped in front of Rick. "What are you still doing here?" His expression irritated, he glanced around the clearing. "And where is that officer? The one who was supposed to escort you out of here?"

"Getting everything I brought you." Even with his hands shoved into his front pockets and his shoulders hunched against the cold, Rick looked at ease.

"We don't need you here." Langley motioned to another officer. "See that Mr. Brady gets to his car."

Jillian had listened to the exchange. Langley wanted Rick Brady gone. That alone—even if she hadn't found Rick's presence comforting—would have been enough to make her speak up.

"I want him here," Jillian said.

The way she figured it, Langley couldn't very well turn down her request, not without appearing cold and heartless. But when she looked at him, she realized that she may have underestimated him. As much as she disliked Detective Langley, he didn't seem all that crazy about her, either. He saw her as a nuisance.

"Stay out of the way, Brady. Or I will have you thrown out of here."

Langley turned and walked to where the two crime-scene officers waited. As they talked in low tones, all three peered into the open ground. What did they see? she wondered. One body or two? Did the grave contain only the body of the woman she and Megan had tried to rescue from the road? Or had they found Megan, too?

Jillian took a sudden sharp breath. She felt as if someone had driven a two-by-four through her sternum and now twisted it, obliterating her heart and lungs. Closing her eyes, trying to gulp air, she fought the pain. It couldn't end like this. Not for her little sister. Not for Megan.

Only hours ago they'd been laughing and teasing each other. And then, only seconds before the accident, Jillian had said that she could leave Megan on the side of the road and never look back. How could she have said those words?

"Enough of this." Rick strode toward Langley. "What do you have?"

Langley took several quick steps to cut off Rick. "Get the hell back!" He jabbed a finger at Rick to emphasize the order.

When Langley immediately turned away, Rick grabbed a handful of the detective's slicker. "A little compassion wouldn't be out of line. Maybe you haven't noticed, but there's a woman standing over here waiting. She's been through enough tonight."

Langley's gaze shifted between Rick and Jillian. He shook off Rick's hand. "Nothing. We're down to undisturbed soil."

Empty.

It took several seconds for Jillian to absorb that. "Empty?" she repeated dully. How was that even possible? She'd listened to the grave being dug. She'd watched the woman be dragged to the back of the truck, the kidnapper's intent obvious.

Numbly, still afraid to believe that it was possible, Jillian walked toward the open ground. She had to see it. Wouldn't believe it until she had seen it with her own eyes. She stopped short of the tarp piled with dirt and looked beyond it and into the three-foot-deep hole.

Empty.

As she looked down at only dirt, the tight knot in her chest eased and she was able to take a deep breath. Megan must be alive.

In the next instant, though, Jillian clenched her eyes and turned away. Alive? The fact that the grave didn't hold Megan, that she hadn't been buried here, guaranteed absolutely nothing. Megan could still be dead.

She felt someone standing just behind her. She couldn't bring herself to turn around. Tears pushed, but she refused to give in to them. She was tough. That's what everyone said about her, even her sister, but she knew that she wasn't tough enough for this. Not for this.

"Come on," Rick said quietly. His hands closed over her shoulders.

She became aware of the activity around them. Officers heading for the road. Langley on the phone again.

"Jillian?" prompted Rick. "There's nothing more you can do here. You need dry clothes. Some sleep."

Yeah. She needed those things. And she would see that she got them. Not because she cared one way or another about being warm, or about sleep. But because she knew that she couldn't afford to collapse. Not until Megan was found.

Jillian looked up at Rick. "What I really need is answers."

She'd had enough of standing by. Of waiting. Of being excluded. She shouldered her way through a group of officers to reach Langley. "What are you doing to find my sister?"

When he seemed intent on ignoring her again, she

grabbed the cell phone anchored to his ear and would have tossed it to the ground if Rick hadn't managed to take it from her.

Langley stepped backward. "Ms. Sorensen. You need to calm down."

"I am calm! Considering my sister is missing. And I can't see that you're doing a hell of a lot about it! Ten minutes. That's how long it would have taken to find out if my sister was buried there. But you wasted more than an hour."

Langley wiped the mist from his tense face. "I understand how hard this is for you. But we're doing everything we can. You need to let us do our jobs." He reclaimed his phone from Rick.

"And I need to know what you're doing. What does *everything you can* really mean, Detective Langley? I have a right to know, don't I? Just as I have the right to know whatever it is that you're keeping from me!"

Instead of answering her, Langley motioned to a female officer. "Ms. Sorensen has a reservation at a B & B on Church Street, the Lancaster House. Make sure that she gets there tonight. And make sure you pick her up in the morning. I want her at the sheriff's office by nine"

Just like that. He was dismissing her. She was to be delivered like some package to the hotel where she and Megan had planned to stay.

It suddenly struck her just how few resources she currently possessed. She had no car, didn't even have any idea what had happened to hers. Langley had assured her there was another group of officers up in the Francis Marion Forest looking for the car, looking for the spot where she and Megan had been abducted. In the meantime, she was without transportation, identification, cash or even credit cards.

Oh sure, a bank account could be accessed, credit cards could be replaced and cars could be rented, but those things would take time. Something else that she was without.

If Megan was alive, then she was in the back of a moving truck. With each passing minute, the search area expanded in concentric circles, the needle becoming smaller as the haystack grew.

When Langley walked away, Rick went after him. "Don't try to make a name for yourself with this one. Call the FBI. Let them have it now. Before it's too late."

Langley rounded on him. "Stay out of it, Brady."

"Like hell I will!"

As Jillian stood there watching the two of them, she realized just how fuzzy her thinking had been for the past hour. She straightened, forced herself to think logically.

Langley liked to run things. So why had he called Rick Brady tonight? What had he wanted from him badly enough to involve Rick?

As Langley turned away, Rick's gaze connected with hers. And more important, why had Rick come out on a night like this? Did he know something? Something that she needed to know?

The female officer who was to drive her to the hotel tried to get her attention. "Ma'am. If you're ready?"

Jillian turned to the woman. "Thanks, but I have a ride."

Chapter Five

Rick watched Jillian Sorensen climb out of his car.

"Thanks again," she said. "For taking me in like this." She paused five feet away, waiting for him, her arms wrapped in front of her, her chin tilted down as if she checked the ground.

"No problem." Rick slid the heavy door to the carriage house closed behind him before turning to her. "It's this way."

He led her toward his house. Because the homes were three stories and had been built close together, the scent of wood smoke from his neighbor's fireplace lingered in the courtyard, mixing with that of wet leaves and the loamy soil of the formal garden.

As with many Charleston yards, it was on the small side and had only a limited grass area—enough for a dog and not enough for children. Two levels of covered porches stretched down one side of the home and served as outside living areas.

She nodded as if in appreciation. "How long have you lived here?"

"Two years."

Jillian climbed the wide set of steps. Rick kept a close eye on her movements, but avoided offering any additional support.

He couldn't quite get a read on her. Most women in her situation would have felt more comfortable with a female cop than a male civilian. Especially one she had just met. So why hadn't Jillian?

Maybe if he hadn't been so busy determining the best way to use the twenty-minute drive to his advantage—he'd been looking for an *in* where the investigation was concerned, and Jillian was the obvious choice——he would have taken the time to question the reason she had asked him for the ride in the first place. But he hadn't.

Just as he had initially failed to question her low-key response to learning that the B & B had given away her room.

Or maybe he'd been too busy counting himself lucky. When he'd heard that she was without a room, he'd offered to let her clean up at his place. He'd expected some hesitation on her part, but to his surprise she'd accepted his offer almost immediately. As if she'd been waiting for the invitation.

Having reached the deck that ran alongside the house, she paused to peel off the plastic shoe cover and, after wadding it up, shoved it into the pocket of the raincoat.

Still silent, she used the edge of the top step to pull off the remaining muddy shoe.

As she undid her coat, he asked, "Have you called anyone back home to let them know?"

During the ride, he'd learned that Jillian and Megan's father had recently passed away, and there were no other relatives, but that obviously didn't eliminate close friends.

"I will in the morning."

As she draped the coat over the banister, he weighed her answer. Either there was no one she felt comfortable calling in the middle of the night, or she was one of those women who didn't easily turn to people, even friends, for help.

The former could play in his favor, while the latter was going to make it difficult to get close to her. To get her to trust him. And he needed to accomplish both of those in a hurry. The next twenty-four to thirty-six hours were going to be the most crucial ones. After that, the odds that the sister would be found plummeted, and along with it that of finding his father's killer.

Even if she didn't know it, they needed each other. For the moment, she had no identification, no transportation and no place to stay. He could provide the last two. And he could help her with Langley, too. And in return, all she had to do was let him help her find her sister.

He pulled his key ring from his pocket. "I hope you don't mind large dogs."

"I'm fine with them."

Another short response. The pattern had been established during the drive. He asked. She answered without hesitation, but in as few words as possible. When she did pose a question, it was one of the generic, socially acceptable ones. Was he married? What did he do now that he wasn't a cop? What she hadn't asked were the ones he would have expected from a woman whose sister had been kidnapped. And that worried him some.

He reached in to turn on the foyer light. Baxter barreled past, hit the top stair and kept going. It wasn't until the golden retriever touched grass that he seemed to realize Rick wasn't alone. By the time the dog sprang around and made the steps again, though, Rick had closed him out.

He watched Jillian take a few steps into the large foyer and look around. In spite of the chandelier, shadows clung to the cove molding overhead and to the corners near the floor. The thick walls created a dense silence. It was one of the things he liked about the home, the sense that just by closing the door, he could lock out the world. Some furniture had come with the house. In the foyer stood a large and ugly antique side table, a painting and two small and useless chairs.

It was the first time that he'd seen Jillian in any kind of real light. Even without makeup, even with the streak of mud that started near her collar and ended just below her left ear, she was damned beautiful. Her dark hair was thick and tangled and fell halfway down her back. With the slicker on, she had appeared small breasted, but she wasn't.

As if aware of his thoughts, she turned away again, seemed to study the landscape painting over the table this time. "I want to know why you were there tonight. Why did Detective Langley call you?"

"Maybe this conversation should wait until after we're cleaned up. I could put some coffee on—"

She faced him. "And stall some more?"

Her directness probably shouldn't have surprised him, but it did. The last time she'd asked, he'd managed to avoid answering, mostly because she'd been preoccupied with what was happening at the time. There were no distractions now, no graves being opened. No way for him to dodge the question.

As much as Rick didn't like Nate Langley, the detective had done the right thing in not mentioning the Midnight Run Murders to Jillian. Even with all the obvious similarities between the two events—the location, the age of most of the victims—to link the two cases prematurely would severely cripple the current investigation.

Not to mention how it would impact her. How would she react when she learned of the fate of the previous victims? How would she feel when she realized that, even after eight years, justice had yet to be served? That the men responsible were still free to take more victims?

But that left Rick with a damn big dilemma. Either tell Jillian the truth—even if it meant pushing her over the edge emotionally—or lose any chance of gaining her trust. It wasn't much of a choice, and he'd made his decision even before she'd asked the question.

"Eight years ago an abandoned truck was found less than a half mile from where we were tonight." He nodded to one of the chairs. "Maybe you should sit down."

"No." She crossed her arms in front of her as if still cold, but he suspected the gesture was more a matter of nerves now.

"My father was the lead investigator." He paused, debating what he was about to say. "The truck was found by a couple of kids who made the mistake of opening up the back end. There were nine women chained inside."

Rick pulled off his ball cap and tossed it into a large bowl on the table. "The temperatures had been in the upper nineties for eight straight days. Given the condition of the bodies, the medical examiner estimated that the truck had been there for at least five of them."

Jillian wobbled backward, sinking into the chair. Though her face remained passive, her eyes didn't. They became darker, more haunted. She had wrapped her hands tightly together in her lap and seemed to study them. "That's what Langley was hiding."

"It's too early to say that there's a connection between the two incidents, but—"

Her gaze connected with his. "But you believe there is."

"I don't believe in coincidences," he said quietly.

Rick wandered to the glass door, stalling. Baxter stood on the other side, tail wagging, eyes hopeful. He ignored the dog, debating how much detail he should go into. Would it be easier for her to have it all at once, or was it better to give her an overview and let other sources provide the hard details? The ones no family member of a victim should ever have to hear?

Right now, her worst nightmare was believing that her sister was chained in the back of a moving truck. As bad as that sounded, it was nothing compared to the truth.

Human trafficking. The selling of women and children as sex slaves into private brothels where they were used over and over again.

Depravity and greed at their worst, and the third most financially lucrative business in the world, ranking close behind weapons and drugs.

What was to become of the captives—of her sister— if they weren't rescued?

If there was one question he hoped to avoid answering tonight, it was that one.

"Tell me the rest," Jillian said.

"The press labeled them the Midnight Run Murders. There wasn't all that much to go on. The truck was stolen just outside Nashville, the plates switched in Georgia. No witness to either event."

Rick shoved his hands into the pockets of his still-damp jeans. "At some point the truck developed mechanical problems. Either the kidnappers attempted to obtain another vehicle, but were unsuccessful, or they simply decided early on to cut their losses. They torched the truck cab before abandoning it. Possibly they had expected the fire to spread to the rest of the vehicle. It didn't."

"There was no—" Jillian broke off. "I assume there were no survivors?" she managed to get out, but her voice shook.

"One—a seventeen-year-old runaway from Orlando. She lasted sixty-two hours, but never regained consciousness. The others were approximately the same age. Attempts to identify them were unsuccessful. The case went cold fairly quickly. No suspects. Little in the way of actual evidence."

For several minutes the only sound was Baxter's quiet whimper and the barely perceptible tinkles of rain hitting gravel.

She forced her shoulder blades against the chair back. "If it had been your father's case, why not call him? Why call you?"

The next words were hard. "Because sixteen months ago my father died. At the time, he was looking into the murders again. It wasn't an official investigation. He'd retired a few months earlier."

Jillian drew a sharp breath. "I'm...sorry."

Rick shrugged, ignoring those words. Partly because

they always sounded so empty when they came from a stranger. "Some men fish in their retirement, others spend their time reading. My father did what he loved. What he did best."

Rick had never completely understood why his father hadn't been able to let it go. But once Jim Brady was diagnosed with lung cancer, Rick had seen the investigation in a different light. It gave his father something to focus on besides his health, besides the timetable given to him by the oncologist.

She glanced down at her hands again. He could see the tension in her knuckles and in the stiffness of her back. "I didn't mean to sound callous." She lifted her chin. "But that still doesn't explain the call to you."

Maybe she was physically exhausted, but mentally she was sharp. He'd been worried that she'd break down on him, that he would be saddled with an emotionally distraught woman, but he realized there was little chance of that happening.

What had made her that tough?

He realized that he was studying her a little too closely again. "Langley called me because I picked up where my father left off."

Her expression remained unyielding. "Why?"

"Officially his death was ruled a suicide. But I believe that he was murdered because of what he was investigating."

She straightened her spine. "You think that if they catch the men who have Megan, you'll find your father's killer, too? Is that why you were out there tonight?"

"Something like that." He knew how cold and self-serving it sounded.

The car heater had dried the mud on Jillian's clothing, and it now flaked onto the rug. She bent to retrieve one of the bigger pieces. "Sorry about the mess. Maybe you should point me toward a shower."

He suspected that her sudden desire to clean up had more to do with the need to be alone.

"Top of the stairs and to the right. Towels are in the cabinet just inside the door. I'll find something for you to put on while your things run through the washer."

At the bottom of the steps, she faced him, her shoulders squared, her chin with a determined tilt. "You were a cop once. What do you think of Langley?"

"He's new to the sheriff's office. I don't know much about him. Except that he closes cases better than most."

Nodding, she reached for the banister. As she climbed the steps, her posture remained stiff. For some reason her rigidity reminded him of a child who'd just been punished but refused to let anyone see her pain.

But he saw it. Just as he saw that Jillian Sorensen was going to be a problem for him. He'd planned to use her, get whatever information she had, then cut her loose. Keeping her close had never entered his mind.

It did now.

Tuesday, 5:16 a.m.

MEGAN WAS MISSING.

Jillian's fingers shook as she tightened the drawstring on the too-large sweatpants. She'd been up for almost twenty-four hours now. Eventually even the adrenaline would fail her and she'd crash. But at least she'd done the right thing in coming here.

Rick believed his father's murder was somehow linked to the men who had her sister. As a former cop, he knew how law enforcement worked, how an investigation was conducted. And he had nearly as much riding on the outcome as she did.

Law school had taught her a lot. How to depose a witness, how to interview a client, how to file motions and cross-examine. How to bill by the hour. But it hadn't taught her anything that was even remotely going to help bring Megan home.

Realizing her breathing had become ragged, she immediately tried to control it. Just as she had been regulating her thoughts and actions for hours now. However, the sense of panic wasn't so easy to manage. Seven years in foster care had taught her how to compartmentalize, taught her to cope, to survive some pretty scary times, but nothing could have prepared her for what she now faced.

Megan was missing.

After jerking the sweatshirt on over her head, Jillian wrapped her clothes in the damp bath towel, then used a strip of toilet tissue to wipe up the worst of the dried mud bits and the fresh blood from the cut on the bottom of her foot. She pulled her wet hair free of the collar, combing it away from her face with her fingers. The mirror was still fogged, but even if it hadn't been, she wouldn't have bothered with it.

She found alcohol, antibiotic cream, tweezers and a box of Band-Aids in the medicine cabinet. She immediately spilled the box into the pedestal sink. She left them there as she peeled back the sweatshirt sleeve covering the injured wrist. Her shower had softened the newly developed scabs to the point that they'd sloughed off, exposing nearly an inch and a half of raw, oozing flesh.

Steeling herself, she dumped alcohol over the wrist. What she needed and didn't have was gauze. So, after applying a layer of antibiotic cream, she just pulled down the sleeve again.

Propping her foot on the closed toilet, she tugged up the left leg of the sweatpants and examined her shin. Only three of the small pellets had actually penetrated flesh. She dribbled alcohol on the tweezers, then her skin. The first two pieces of shot came out easily, but the third gave her more problems.

By the time she was done, blood trickled from the site. More alcohol and then antibiotic cream. She ripped open half a dozen Band-Aids, applying them to her shin and the bottom of her right foot. The remaining scrapes and cuts were going to have to wait.

Megan was missing.

Gathering up the wrappers, she flung them into the wastebasket and then shoved the other items back into the medicine cabinet. She still had to make phone calls. She needed a duplicate driver's license and an ATM card as quickly as possible, and at least one credit card. Without them, she couldn't rent a car or get a hotel room. Come daylight, she'd see about hiring a private investigator. Maybe two. Rick would probably know people.

In the meantime she needed to convince him that they should team up. Which wouldn't be easy if he discovered that she'd tricked him into bringing her back here. When she'd asked to borrow his cell phone to call the hotel, she had instead dialed her own cell number and acted as if her reservation had been canceled.

Maybe it was a bit of a gamble, but she had to go with her gut instinct. His actions tonight had suggested that he wasn't the kind of guy to leave a woman in her situation stranded. He'd step up and do the right thing. Of course, if he discovered he'd been lied to…

Megan was missing, and Jillian didn't care what it took. She was going to get her back. She'd lie, steal and even commit murder if she had to. Nothing was going to stop her.

Jillian opened the bathroom door. So where was Rick? Still showering? Making coffee? Checking his phone log? Discovering her deceit? God, she was such a pathetic liar.

Warm, moist air spilled out into the dim hallway. Like those downstairs, the floors on the second level were a mahogany color and had been left bare. But because of the stark white walls and high ceiling, the space felt more like a contemporary loft than a historic home.

Jillian reached for the banister. Where was Megan right now? What was happening to her? And what would happen to her, to the other women, when the truck reached its destination? As much as Jillian had wanted to ask Rick all those questions, something inside had kept her silent. Maybe it was because deep down she already knew the truth. And couldn't handle hearing it spoken aloud. What else could it be but white slavery? Why else would men chain women like animals in the back of a truck? She'd watched the news specials. Women sold like livestock, forced into brothels, used over and over again until they were used up.

Halfway down the stairs her vision blurred. Her chest tightened. She couldn't breath. Another few steps and she plopped down hard, tears starting to flow un-checked. She wiped at them with both hands. She couldn't afford to break down now. Tears didn't solve a damn thing. Megan needed her. Just as the victims eight years ago had needed someone to rescue them.

Nine women left to suffocate in the back of a truck.

Still gripping the railing, afraid to let it go, she rested her forehead against the cool plaster. How could that happen? How could something so barbaric…? Why hadn't someone been made to pay?

She swiped at her tears. Those nine women had all been someone's child. They hadn't been brought into the world to be disposable.

More tears… And then she was thinking about her own mother. About how no one had claimed her mother's body from the morgue twenty-one years ago. How no one had come forward to claim her, either.

Alone.

Throughout the seven years in foster care she'd always felt so damn alone. Until the Sorensens. Until Megan.

She was bawling now, her shoulders heaving, her nose running. Image after image came after her in a relentless progression. Her mother's body being wheeled out of the cheap hotel room. Megan reading a road map. The burned-out shell of a truck parked in a clearing. The horror inside. Megan turning to her in the car, a smart remark on her lips. The terrified look in her eyes as she begged Jillian to leave her.

She'd left her sister. What kind of monster was she?

When warm hands grasped her shoulders, she jerked as if to escape, but then turned and plunged blindly into Rick. He caught her, his arms closing around her.

He was a stranger.

She didn't care.

She needed something to hold on to, and he was hard and solid. Over and over her fingers twisted into his sweatshirt. If she could just get closer, maybe she wouldn't feel so damned scared, so damned alone. But she knew better. She was supposed to feel those things.

"It was my fault that we were on that road tonight. If I had been paying more attention…" She tried to swallow, but couldn't. "Me. It should have been me. Not Megan!"

He held on to her. "We don't get to choose. We just get to cope."

"I left her there in the back of that truck." What if she hadn't been thinking about saving her sister's life when she'd plunged into those woods? What if she'd actually been thinking about her own survival? What if Megan was wrong about her? What if even after all the years of her adopted family's kindness and love, she really was damaged goods?

"You did the right thing, Jillian. And at times doing the right thing is hard as hell. Staying wouldn't have helped your sister or those other women. Escaping means they have a possibility of being rescued."

She lifted her chin. "But I promised to protect her."

"You couldn't."

Rick pushed her damp hair away from her face and then used his fingers to wipe away tears. "What you're doing now—blaming yourself—we all do that. It's natural when something happens to the people we love. But it doesn't make it true." He tipped her chin up, forcing her to meet his gaze. "We'll find her. You have to believe that."

She didn't believe him. She wasn't that naive.

"Like they found them eight years ago?"

"They have more to go on this time. They have everything from the previous investigation. And they have you."

"Me? I don't know anything. I don't know what color the truck was, or if it had printing on the side." She hiccuped. "I didn't even check the damn license plate."

"But you can identify your kidnappers. You saw their faces."

Chapter Six

Megan banged her head against the side of the truck over and over in an attempt to stay awake. She ignored the small voice inside that suggested it was a misguided attempt to quell her fear. Small voices inside her head meant she was losing it, right?

I'll be back for you. No matter what. Jillian. How long had it been since her sister's escape? Since they'd rolled down the back door and gone after her?

Megan's attempts to rouse the other captives had been futile. If she had to guess, the other women had been here longer, had probably been drugged more frequently.

Is that what would happen to her? Would she eventually be reduced to a catatonic state? Where she had no hope of fighting back? Of escaping? She had to fight it! She had to stay awake.

She'd tried counting, but immediately lost track. Whatever they'd given her was meant to dull her senses, and for the most part it did. Everything but the fear.

If Jillian didn't make it, Megan knew *she* wouldn't, either.

They'd left a light on this time. It wasn't much of one, just enough to break the gloom. And to allow Megan to see the other captives.

In their haste, the kidnappers had left the woman from the road just inside the back door. She was on her stomach, her face turned away. The arm that she'd been dragged by remained outstretched, almost as if she were reaching out to Megan.

Was she already dead? Megan's fingers curled in trepidation.

She'd sat by her father's bedside for hours after he'd been pronounced dead, his fingers cooling beneath her touch despite her best efforts to keep them warm. Death was cold and stiff and terrifyingly empty.

But what if the woman was still alive? Megan reached out. At first contact, she jerked back. Cool to the touch, but still too warm to be dead. *She was alive.* Barely. Megan tugged the woman's hand closer.

"You're not alone," Megan whispered, but didn't know whether the words were meant to comfort herself or to give hope to the stranger. Maybe it didn't matter.

She rested her head in the straw and, closing her eyes, pretended that the hand she held was Jillian's. And that they were sharing a bed as they had when they were younger. Jillian had always been there for her…always.

Sometime later a loud clanking noise woke her up. For a moment she was disoriented. She'd been dreaming about camping out in the backyard. Blinking, she tried to clear her head, but the effort didn't seem worth the expenditure of energy.

Allowing her eyes to drift closed again, she mumbled, "So cold, Jilly."

Megan reached down for her blanket. As she did, the chain rattled overhead. It was that sound that finally managed to break through. A harsh whimper escaped before she could stop it, and her eyes shot wide open, her hand tightening on the other woman's.

A flashlight beam bounced around the interior briefly before the taller of the two kidnappers stepped up into the space. No sign of Jillian. She lowered her eyelids and watched the man.

His hair was reddish and shaggy, but he was the kind of man that some women would find appealing. He wore a T-shirt and a denim jacket. Mud covered the bottom of his jeans. The clothes hadn't been clean even before the mud, though, and smelled of both old sweat and new.

As desperately as she wanted to look toward the back opening, Megan forced herself to remain motionless. Where was the other man, and why hadn't the two of them returned together? Because they'd split up? Because one went to chase Jillian, while the other came back to kill and bury the woman from the road?

The man started whistling, same as before. As if kidnapping and murder were nothing. He bent over the other woman and grabbed her ankle. Everything inside Megan rebelled. She tightened her grip on the woman's hand. She wouldn't let go. She'd hold on tight.

But with the first tug, the connection was broken, and as soon as it was, something went cold inside Megan. Alone again. With nothing to hold on to but fear.

She waited, using sound to track the action around

her. Instead of hoisting the woman out the back door as Megan had expected, the man dragged her deeper into the truck. Opening her eyes to slits, Megan watched the woman's body gouging a trail through the straw.

Why the change in plans?

Megan's pulse hammered. Maybe they couldn't follow through with their plans to get rid of the woman because Jillian had escaped and would be able to lead the cops back to their current location. Leaving a body behind would be too risky, wouldn't it?

Had Jillian made it, then? Was it possible that her sister had already found help? That the nightmare would end before the night did? What other explanation could there be? Hope swelled in her chest.

The man's continued whistling crushed it. He didn't seem overly anxious about Jillian's escape. Didn't seem in a hurry. Was it because their location was so remote and he assumed they had plenty of time before the cops arrived?

He left the woman near the front wall of the truck, facedown with her legs splayed behind her. Before he could turn around, Megan again closed her eyes, pretending that she'd fallen into the same semicomatose state as the other captives.

She again relied upon sound to track his movements. The rattle of chain just to the right of where he'd left the woman, the rustle of straw shifting underfoot as he moved from one victim to the next.

Fear and panic surged as he squatted down in front of her. She could feel his gaze. She tried to keep breathing slow and easy, but in a matter of seconds she was sucking in at least some air through parted lips.

Something cool and hard brushed across the back of the fisted fingers of her right hand. Once. Twice. It took everything in her not to flinch, to leave her hand exposed. It was as if she held it within the jaws of a lethal trap that could at any moment spring closed, severing it.

"Come on. Let me see those pretty eyes."

This time, as he dragged the item across her hand, she decided it was some type of small chain. Maybe a necklace or something.

The item—a piece of jewelry—was withdrawn. "I got something for you. Just open your eyes and I'll show you."

She kept them closed.

The rasp of a zipper.

As his fingers brushed the top button of her blouse, she threw her upper torso up and backward. Her spine and head crashed into the metal wall. The air trapped in her lungs exploded free. Like an oxygen-deprived diver who has just reached the surface, she gulped in more. Her feet scrambled. She couldn't immediately find traction in the slippery straw, but after many attempts, she managed to get both ankles in tight beneath her buttocks. She kept her hands raised, ready to fend off attempts to touch her.

"I knew you were awake. Watching me. Bet you wondered what I'd do next." Smiling, he ran his jacket zipper up and down a final time and then released it. "We can either make this easy or we can make it hard."

She had no idea what he referred to. But she suspected that at the very least it involved rape.

Watching him cautiously, she tried to determine his next move. Out of the corner of her eye, she saw a hint of movement just outside the back door. The momentary loss of concentration left her vulnerable. The man in front of her grabbed her left ankle and jerked it from beneath her.

She kicked out with her other foot. The blow connected with his rib cage. In retaliation, his fist slammed into her jaw, driving the back of her skull into the wall.

Dazed now, Megan watched him pull a small bottle of water from his jacket pocket. Uncapping it, he moved in closer.

"Consider that lesson one. Buyers don't want damaged goods, but that won't stop me. You either do as you're told, or there are consequences." He held out the bottle to her, indicating that she should drink.

Was he really offering her water? It seemed unlikely. But did it really matter?

As he pressed the opening to her lips, they parted. Closing her eyes, she took a large sip. As soon as it hit her tongue, she knew that it was laced with something bitter. She swallowed it anyway.

Maybe being out of it wasn't such a bad thing. She wasn't Jillian. She didn't know how to pick a lock. Wasn't very good at fighting back. She'd never had to, she realized, because Jillian had always been there to do it for her.

He shoved the bottle into one pocket and pulled a camera out of the other. Seeing it, she turned toward the metal mesh in an effort to hide her face. He jerked her back around and ripped open her blouse.

Tuesday, 9:03 a.m.

RICK WATCHED the activity out in the hallway. Despite the thick glass, the sounds of a busy sheriff's office penetrated the interview room where Langley had left them nearly ten minutes ago.

The room was average in size and hadn't changed since the last time Rick had been in it. Dark carpeting, beige walls. A conference table occupied the center of the room and was surrounded by six chairs.

At the moment Jillian sat with her legs crossed at the knees and her hands folded in her lap. The picture of patience, if you could ignore the way one foot constantly jiggled.

She'd changed back into her own clothes. They might have been good quality at one time, but a trip through the washer and dryer had pretty much destroyed them. The athletic shoes that she wore had been borrowed from his next-door neighbor, and the too-large black leather bomber jacket that now hung over her chair was his.

The door opened. Langley shouldered his way in, trying to hold on to three cups of coffee. "Sorry to take so long."

The detective wore the same slacks and shoes as the night before. But now he'd changed into a fresh blue oxford-cloth shirt, and his head was slightly damp, as if he'd dunked it into a sink.

As Langley nudged the door closed with his foot, his gaze met Rick's. The look in the detective's eyes confirmed what Rick had been sensing since their arrival here this morning. Something was up.

Jillian pulled the cup of coffee Langley put in front of her closer. As she lifted it to her lips, her hand shook. She lowered it slowly. As soon as the cup bottom touched the table, her shoulders rose and fell.

Most people probably wouldn't have noticed the habit. He did. Every time she exhibited some outward sign that she wasn't in complete control, she would stop and take a deep breath. He studied her, analyzing without a second thought. Control was important to her. He suspected that the image of being in control was even more crucial. Which was why her complete break-down on the stairs had taken him by surprise.

He'd just hung up from the phone conversation with the bed-and-breakfast, having learned that she'd lied to him. A room was still being held in her name. He'd intended to confront her…. Instead he'd held her in his arms.

That's when he'd realized that Jillian Sorensen was his least favorite kind of woman—complicated.

He watched as she picked up her cup. This time she managed to take a quick sip. Like Langley and himself, she was functioning on too little sleep and too much caffeine.

Most women would have looked like hell. She didn't. She had high cheekbones, a feminine cleft in her chin. Her eyes—a gold-green color—stared out from beneath strong brows that were a slightly deeper brown than her hair. The dark circles beneath her eyes spoke of exhaustion. How much longer could she stay on her feet?

Langley placed another cup, obviously intended for Rick, just to the left of Jillian. "Normally I try to exclude friends and family, but given your familiarity with the case, you may be able to add something."

Rick wondered what had happened overnight. Why the detective seemed so much more agreeable this morning.

Langley took his seat. "I just ran into Special Agents Durwood and McDaniel out in the hall. They'll be here shortly."

The news that the FBI had been brought in sharpened Rick's attention. It was probably the reason Langley had cleaned up. And the reason he was more cooperative, too.

Rick pulled out the chair next to Jillian. "Has the abduction site or Jillian's car been located?"

"I have a team processing the scene now. We got lucky with the weather, though. The rain bands bypassed the area, which means we were able to locate several small amounts of blood on the pavement. Most likely it will belong to Jillian and the woman she and her sister were trying to help, and not one of our perps." He rubbed his face. "There's been no sign of the car yet. Or of a shotgun casing. Forty yards to the west of the scene, we located an area where two vehicles had been pulled back into the trees."

"Was there a match to the tracks at the other scene?"

"Yes."

"What about the second set? Any indication of the type of vehicle?"

"Not a truck. Definitely smaller. Beyond that…"

Jillian spoke up. "Any possibility that it was my car that made them?"

"Sure." Langley took a sip of his own coffee. "There are several service stations within a ten-mile radius. Officers are questioning the employees and pulling any videos from surveillance cameras. It's a long shot, but…"

Rick knew what Langley was doing—justifying his own performance to date. He would retain control of the investigation to a certain degree, but now that the FBI was involved, a task force would be created composed of local, state and federal law enforcement.

The door opened, two men stepping into the room. Both wore suits and carried notebooks, but that was where the similarity ended. One man was six-four or so with a rangy build, the other man nearly half a foot shorter. Despite the taller one's silver hair, Rick put his age somewhere in his late forties. He was the first to speak.

"Good morning." Special Agent Thomas Durwood made quick introductions, then sat opposite Jillian, leaving Special Agent McDaniel the chair across from Rick.

That the special agents didn't question his presence indicated that Langley had briefed them, making Rick curious what had been said.

For the next twenty minutes, Durwood and McDaniel interviewed Jillian, forcing her to retrace every moment of the kidnapping and her escape. Did she get a look at her kidnappers? How close? What about the woman she and her sister had tried to rescue? The other victims chained in the back of the truck? What did she think the average age was? Teens? Twenties? Most of the information would be in Langley's notes, but the feds usually insisted on doing their own thing.

Occasionally Langley would jump in with a comment, usually addressed to Durwood, confirming that the two men had discussed the case to some degree, probably by phone.

As Jillian had spoken, Durwood had jotted down bullet points of information. "Is there anything else you can think of?"

She fiddled with her nearly empty cup, her fingers rotating it while it still sat on the table in front of her. "One of the men was from around here."

"Why do you say that?" Langley asked.

"I grew up in Charleston," she offered without looking up. "His accent… He was from around here."

Rick's gaze flickered between Langley and the two agents. Jillian's announcement surprised Rick but not the others. Why? Because they'd known? It was hard to remain mute. On the other hand, it wasn't Rick's place to ask questions. Not now.

Ten more minutes into the interview and a deputy entered and motioned Langley out of the room. Moments later Langley returned.

"Your convertible has just been pulled out of a small lake just to the east of the abduction site." Reclaiming his seat, he continued, "The trunk contained your three suitcases, but neither purse was found."

"The top was down." Jillian rubbed her head. "My purse was behind my seat. Megan's, too."

Langley nodded. "They may have been swept out as the car submerged. We're still looking. The water's murky, so it may take some time for the divers to search the lake bottom completely."

Durwood made a note. "Just in case the kidnapper took the purses, I'll have the activity checked on the credit cards." He looked toward Langley. "Who's processing the car?"

"Our lab," Langley said. "As soon as the vehicle

dries out, they'll try to pull some latent prints. We can probably get a set of elimination prints for Megan from the inside of one of the suitcase." Langley glanced over at Jillian. "And we'll get yours here in a few minutes. In the meantime, I have an artist on his way in to work with you on some drawings of the kidnappers."

She nodded.

Langley glanced at Durwood. "I think that about does it for now."

"What about getting a sketch of the woman they tried to rescue?" Rick suggested. "She doesn't fit the profile of their other victims. She's older, and she obviously isn't a runaway. She was wearing a business suit. Maybe she's a businesswoman."

Jillian sat forward. "A southern one."

"What makes you say that?" Durwood's eyes narrowed.

"The color of her suit," Jillian went on. "Not many northern women wear pastel colors this time of year."

"We've checked and no one fitting the woman's description has been reported missing," Langley said.

"It's Thanksgiving week," Rick pressed. "Even if a neighbor or friend has noticed her absence, they may assume she's visiting out-of-town family. Or maybe her job requires her to travel. Take her picture national, someone will recognize her. It might give us another crime scene. Maybe a better one. It may also give us an idea of their route."

Durwood zipped closed the soft-sided leather binder. "Mr. Brady has a point. Just because the abduction took place north of Charleston and the second scene is to the south, we shouldn't assume they are headed in that direction. A collaborating piece of evidence, like this woman's identity and the location of her abduction, may help us determine with more certainty."

Langley frowned. "Three sketches, then." He turned to Jillian. "If you'll follow me we can get your prints."

Rick started to rise. Durwood caught his attention. "If you've got a minute?"

As soon as Langley and Jillian left, Durwood stood and said, "Follow me."

They moved to the interview room just across the hall. As in the room he'd just left, the blinds at the window remained open. Because the contents of the cardboard file box he'd delivered to Langley hours earlier covered the table, Rick assumed Durwood wanted to discuss them.

"I believe Detective Langley has arranged for a set of copies. If you have no objections, I'd like to retain the originals."

Rick took the seat Durwood indicated. He'd brought his untouched coffee with him. "I would prefer to keep the originals."

If Durwood thought the request unusual, he gave no indication of it. "Was there a reason why your father decided to take another look at the murders?"

"He was a cop. Retirement didn't change that."

Recognizing the red folder in the middle of the table, Rick flipped it open. The photo on top had been taken from outside the truck, looking into the back end of it. It wasn't the best shot—mostly shadows, except for the single sliver of sunshine that cut a swath five or six feet into the interior. But there in the pool of light was an object encased in a steel manacle. A barely recognizable human wrist and hand.

Rick sat back. "I don't imagine anyone who really worked on the case can completely forget it."

Durwood nodded. "I've gone through everything. There are no recent notes made by your father."

"He kept them with him. In a small notebook."

"Is there some reason you didn't turn it over with the rest?"

"It's not in my possession."

"Who does have it?"

Rick leaned forward. "I couldn't tell you. Maybe whoever murdered him."

"Langley mentioned that you don't think your father's death was a suicide. Any idea who would kill a terminally ill man?"

"I think he got too close to someone."

"What about you?" Durwood rubbed his face. "Have you turned up anything that isn't in the notes you provided to Detective Langley?"

"Unfortunately, no. Without the notebook, I've been forced to go back to the original investigation, try to second-guess what my father saw when he reexamined it."

Durwood flipped the cover closed on the file folder containing the photos and reached for another one, sorting it from the pile on his left. He placed it in front of him. "How much has Ms. Sorensen told you about her background?"

"We haven't had any long conversations, if that's what you mean."

"Did she tell you that she's adopted?"

"No. Of course not."

"She was born right here in Charleston. First entered foster care at the age of five. She was briefly reunited with her mother for a period of three months, during which time her mother was murdered. Some kids do well in the system. Jillian didn't. Five homes in seven years. The Sorensens were the sixth. They adopted her."

Where in the hell was Durwood going with any of this? "And?"

"Just prior to the adoption, a psychologist examined her. He felt that Jillian's inability to trust was a stumbling block to her forming lasting relationships."

"I'm no expert, but everything I've seen suggests that Jillian is fully bonded to Megan." Rick was quickly losing patience. He didn't have time for this bull. And neither did Durwood.

Durwood pulled several sheets of paper out from beneath the one he was reading. He slid them across the table to Rick, then closed the file cover. "If something happens to her sister, Jillian Sorensen stands to inherit a sizable estate. And if you start taking the evidence piece by piece, all we have so far is an empty grave, tire tracks and a car that's been driven into a lake.

"And Jillian Sorensen's story?"

"What if everything she's told us is a lie?"

"So you think it's possible that Jillian got rid of her sister? And then came up with this elaborate story?" Rick stood. "Does Langley subscribe to this theory? Because you are way off base here. Jillian had me contact a private investigator for her this morning."

"What better way to divert suspicion?" Durwood retrieved the pages and shoved them back into the folder. "I can't afford not to consider all angles."

"Just because Jillian's start in life wasn't the best doesn't mean that she's capable of harming her sister."

"The case will be worked like any other kidnapping. I just want you to be aware that the woman you've taken in may not be the innocent victim that she claims to be."

Rick tossed the coffee cup into the trash can. "I know emotional devastation when I see it."

"Yeah? What about guilt? Sometimes it's not so easy to nail down. What if she's done something to her sister and now feels guilty about it?"

"So why not ask her about it?"

Durwood glanced toward the adjacent room. Through the open blinds Rick's gaze connected with Jillian's. The shell-shocked look on her face confirmed that McDaniel and Langley were presenting the same scenario Durwood just had.

She'd been through too much already. What she was being forced to listen to was inhumane.

The special agent's smug look was more than Rick could take. Leaning down, he planted his knuckles on the table. "You son of a bitch. Less than twelve hours ago she was chained up next to her sister. Without her courage, you wouldn't have squat."

Rick straightened. "You're wrong about her. Very wrong."

Chapter Seven

Jillian followed the waitress up the restaurant's steep stairs. Though still early for lunch, there was already a line outside Higgins Seafood. The restaurant, which dated back to the early fifties, was located in the heart of Charleston's historic district.

There was nothing fancy about Higgins. The floor was worn vinyl, the tables the original ones, and a peek into the kitchen would probably end all desire to eat. For all that, Higgins was still an area icon.

The table they were shown to was a corner one on the second level. Jillian chose a chair where her back would be to the room. Maybe it was silly. It wasn't as if she would run into anyone who knew her. But the truth was that she found it difficult to face even strangers right now.

Maybe it was just as well that the artist hadn't been able to get there this morning, had needed to reschedule for twelve-thirty. It gave Jillian time to regroup, to pull herself together. There was a lot riding on the sketches. It was the only thing she had to contribute right now and deep down she was panicked that she wouldn't get it right. For Megan's sake, they had to be perfect.

Jillian placed the new cell phone on the table. After leaving the sheriff's office, they'd made two stops— one to replace the phone, the other to pick up necessities. She'd grabbed slacks, jeans, a couple of sweaters and some sensible shoes without even trying the first of them on.

She had wanted to wait until the replacement credit and ATM cards arrived tomorrow, but her own clothes were beyond ruined. As much as she disliked borrowing money from Rick, she hated the way people stared even more.

Somehow it felt almost surreal, as if she were living parallel lives—one fictional, one terrifyingly real. In the fictional one, phone calls were made, toothbrushes and panties were purchased. But in the other one, the real one, her sister was missing, the Feds thought her capable of murder and she felt powerless to change any of it.

Rick settled in the chair opposite. He looked relaxed and comfortable. She was neither. When he'd suggested eating here, she'd thought she'd be okay, but now she realized it was going to be much tougher than she'd imagined.

Rick pushed the paper menu aside. "Have you been here before?"

"Yes. We used to come in almost weekly before we moved. It was my adoptive mother's favorite restaurant."

Jillian grabbed a peanut from the bowl in the center of the table. "I'm sure the last time I had boiled peanuts it was here." She peeled off the soft shell, popped the peanut into her mouth.

Rick selected one for himself. "I suppose they're hard to get in Ohio?"

"Yes. Grits are a little easier."

"So you like Southern foods?"

"Mostly." She wiped her hands on the napkin. "Don't death-penalty lawyers have appointments to keep?"

Because she'd been expecting him to dump her at the bed-and-breakfast when they'd left the sheriff's office, it had taken her by surprise when he'd pushed to have the artist come to his place later. What were Rick's intentions where she was concerned? At what point was he going to bail on her?

Last night he'd indicated that he thought his father's murder was somehow linked to what was happening now, but he hadn't really offered any details. Did he believe one of the kidnappers was the killer? If that was the case, once she did the sketch, wouldn't he have all that he needed from her?

He looked up from where he was selecting another peanut. "If at all possible, I don't schedule appointments the week of Thanksgiving, and I take off the second half of December."

"Sounds like a great schedule."

He discarded the shell, adding it to the growing pile on a second small plate. "The holidays are tough on my clients and on their families. This time of year everyone starts to regret everything. And to be honest, I find it hard to deal with."

Wiping his mouth, Rick sat back. "So you were going to interview with Burroughs, Alderson & Bailey?"

They'd talked about it in the car last night. "Do you know anything about them?"

"I'm sure you've already heard that they're one of the larger firms in Charleston. Lots of high-profile cases involving international law. Did you reschedule the interview?"

"No." She couldn't think about the future. Not until she knew what it held. Not until Megan was safe.

Jillian opened the menu the hostess had left. She tried to read it, but the printing blurred as tears threatened to fill her eyes. How could anyone think that she would hurt Megan? It was insanity.

Reflexively, Jillian touched her throat, her cool fingers spreading, momentarily searching for the delicate gold chain that wasn't there. Even the smallest of familiarities were gone now.

As Jillian lowered her hand, Rick caught it. The contact shocked her. It was as if she'd dipped frostbitten fingers into warm water.

She let her eyes drift to his. He held her fingers for several seconds, his gaze probing hers. What did he see? Someone who could harm her sister? The possibility scared her more than it should have, she realized.

"You do that a lot. Touch your throat. As if you're searching for something."

Her fingers curled as she withdrew them. "My adoptive mother gave me a necklace. It had been her grandmother's." Jillian pretended to glance down at the menu. "I always wore it as a reminder."

"Of what?"

She looked up. "That I'd hit the jackpot. Gotten what every kid wants. Security. Love. A chance to thrive."

"Where is it now?"

"Either it came off during the struggle or it was taken from me when I was unconscious." She closed the menu. "What did Durwood tell you? About me?"

"That you didn't have an easy time of it before the Sorensens."

She laughed, the sound brittle to her own ears. "That's an understatement." The Sorensens had been warm and open and loving. Some of the other foster families had been that way, also. Unfortunately, not all of them had. The first twelve years of her life hadn't made it easy to trust.

She knew Rick was holding back. His answer had been too…polite. How much had Durwood told Rick about her background? She couldn't think of any reason the special agent would hold back. But had he given Rick the down-and-dirty version—told him how at age five she'd been found clinging to her mother's dead body in a room that was rented by the hour? That there was no father's name on her birth certificate?

She dropped her hands into her lap. Maybe it didn't matter what Durwood had said. She couldn't change where she came from. And she'd stopped apologizing for it a long time ago. Maybe she and Rick just needed to get what McDaniel and Durwood had said out in the open. Wouldn't it be better to know where she stood with Rick?

She started to reach up for the missing necklace again, but managed to stop herself midmotion. "Agent McDaniel asked a lot of questions about my relationship with Megan. If something happens to her, I…um…" She laced her hands together and squeezed. "I never expected to be named in the will. They loved me like a daughter, but I wasn't."

"The questions that McDaniel asked were meant to eliminate you as a suspect. Those closest to the victim always come under scrutiny."

"We both know that's not true. If my background was different, if I was Megan's biological sister…"

"Doing that to yourself is nonproductive. Trust me, I know."

"I appreciate all you've done," she began, and then hesitated before adding, "I don't think I could have gotten through any of this without you."

"Yes, you would have. And don't give me too much credit here. I got involved for my own selfish reasons. I want answers, answers I think you can help me get. In exchange I'll do everything I can to find your sister." Rick leaned forward, resting his elbows on the table. "What do you say? Do you want to team up? Can you trust me, Jillian? Can you let me in?"

On the face of things, his proposition seemed quite simple. Only, it didn't feel that way.

He waited for her answer.

"I don't know," she said after several more seconds.

He confused her. She confused herself. Let him in? He was more than halfway there. Last night she'd barely noticed how attractive he was, but today it wasn't so easy to ignore. He was dressed in khaki slacks and a white oxford shirt. His eyes were gray and there was a directness in them that she found disconcerting and comforting at the same time.

"Do you need to hear me say that I don't buy that you're involved in your sister's disappearance?"

Was she that transparent?

His fingers reached for hers. "I don't."

Tuesday 12:14 p.m.

THE PHONE STARTED ringing as Rick unlocked the front door. Jillian followed him in. By the time she got the door closed and locked behind them, she was feeling jittery. Maybe there was news. Maybe they'd found Megan.

Rick had left the file box he'd been carrying on the entry table. As the phone rang again, Jillian dropped the sacks of clothing on a side chair and chased after him, stopping when she reached the kitchen doorway.

The space obviously hadn't been updated. White cabinets from sometime in the forties or fifties were in need of demolition or paint. The wallpaper depicted fruit. The only saving grace was windows overlooking the courtyard.

As if he understood just how anxious she was, Rick glanced at her just before picking up the handset.

She folded her arms in front of her, tightening them as she desperately tried to read his face. *Please don't let it be bad news.*

After the briefest of moments, Rick's gaze found hers and he shook his head. She would have expected the pressure in her chest to ease some. It didn't.

It had been a rough night, and in some ways a rougher morning. As much as she didn't want to admit it, the way other people saw her still affected the way she viewed herself.

For so much of her life, the mirror placed in front of her had shown a neglected child, one with little hope of attaining happiness. It had been the Sorensens who had held up a different sort of mirror. In it, she had seen a young girl with gifts and talents. She'd worked hard to get where she was today—not physically, and maybe not even so much intellectually, but certainly emotionally. And in a matter of minutes, she'd allowed two federal agents to take it all away from her.

She needed to be stronger, damn it. She loved Megan, would give her life for her little sister. And whether anyone besides Megan believed that didn't matter.

Jillian started to turn away, but something in Rick's expression stopped her.

He appeared irritated as he grabbed the message pad next to the phone and scribbled something. Dropping the handset back onto the base, he tore off the top sheet. "Baxter's gotten out. And if we don't get him now, they're going to call animal control."

He glanced at his watch. She knew he was thinking about the artist who was due in fifteen minutes, debating if there was enough time for them to get there and back. Torn between what he considered to be two responsibilities.

"Why don't you go on. I'll wait for the artist." She could sense that he didn't want to leave her behind, and maybe there was a part of her that didn't want him to, but she wasn't going to give in to it. "I'll be fine," she reassured him again and smiled.

"Okay." He jotted something on the pad. "Here's my cell number. If you need anything, call."

She followed him to the front door.

"I should be back by the time the artist gets here. But if I'm not, ask to see some identification before you let him in." He opened the door. "And lock this behind me."

She watched him jog down the front steps. It had started to rain again, the sky the same dirty gray cement color as Ohio's this time of year. Even the yellow mums in pots at the bottom of the steps seemed washed out.

As he pulled open the driver's door of his SUV, he looked back. She smiled, offered a wave. He did the same.

For the first time since the attack, she was alone. And she didn't like it. Jillian finally threw the dead bolt and turned her back to the door. Even after what he'd said in the restaurant about working together, it wouldn't be a good idea to start counting on Rick Brady too much.

As she passed the entry table, the file box caught her attention. Pausing, she ran a hand over the closed top. Rick hadn't said anything when he'd carried it out of the sheriff's office. But even with no label on the exterior, she knew what was inside—information about the case his father had worked on. The Midnight Run Murders.

Last night he'd been very cautious with what he'd told her about the murders. He'd assumed that she couldn't handle it. But wouldn't it be better to know what was in the box, no matter how bad it was? Wasn't it always easier to cope with the known than the unknown?

Still uneasy with her decision, she lifted off the lid. There was a musty scent, as if the box had spent some time in a damp spot. There were hanging files, most of them with tabs indicating their contents—medical examiner reports, physical evidence, preliminary reports.

She pulled out the first of them and flipped it open. Inside was a stack of photos, the edges worn from handling. The top one depicted a burned-out truck cab, the next a woodsy clearing where sunshine poured through the overhead canopy—a scene that could have made a South Carolina travel brochure. She took a deep, steadying breath. It would be difficult to distinguish this clearing from the one last night, the only obvious differences the season and the time of day.

As she flipped to the next photo, she bobbled the file. The back doors to the truck stood open now, and there was just enough light that she could make out the shadowed outline of two bodies. Her throat tightened as if she were being choked. She sagged against the wall, suddenly needing the support. This was death. This was what could happen to her sister. This was what could be happening right now to Megan.

She couldn't get the damn file out of her hands fast enough. Knowledge didn't always guarantee power. Sometimes it just revealed how damn powerless you really were.

Someone knocked on the front door. Startled, she briefly lost control of the file and several photos slipped out and onto the floor. She dropped to her knees and desperately scraped them together with hands and fingers that were still shaking so badly that she couldn't seem to make them work.

More pounding, this time accompanied by a male voice on the other side of the door. "Charleston County Sheriff's."

Everything inside her went cold all over again. Because she'd been expecting him, she'd assumed it would be the artist. But what if he wasn't? What if he was a deputy delivering news?

"I'm coming." Her heart slamming hard and fast, she dumped the pictures on the table facedown. At the last second, remembering Rick's words, she threw on the security chain, then opened the door.

The man standing there obviously wasn't a deputy. Probably a freelance artist. He wasn't overly tall, either—five-eight or so. Dark hair. Late twenties, maybe early thirties. While the heavy-framed glasses made him appear artsy, the conservative black raincoat gave the impression that he was older. The black baseball cap was pulled low, making it seem as if he had no forehead.

"Jillian Sorensen? Brian Balthrop." He lifted the brown leather artist portfolio slightly.

"Can I see some identification?"

Looking slightly perturbed, he presented a photo ID. After studying it, she let him in.

By the time Jillian turned from relocking the door, he stood halfway to the front stairs. Odd, she thought. Most people, when invited into an unfamiliar house, waited close to the entrance.

She walked toward him, intending to take his raincoat. A small frisson of nerves went through her, and at first she reasoned it away. She'd been victimized. Unfamiliar men were bound to set her on edge. Even those who shouldn't.

She stopped three feet from him, having noticed the brown leather gloves. Despite the nasty weather, it was too warm for gloves, especially these. They were shooting gloves, the leather ultrathin.

Why would an artist wear shooting gloves? Unless…he wasn't who he said he was. She suddenly understood the reason he'd moved away from the door. To force her away from it, too.

What did he want? To kill her? Why else would he

be here? Her heart was beating triple time, and her flesh felt cold. Her hand started to creep to her throat, but she caught herself in time. She couldn't afford to look nervous. He'd know that she was on to him.

Think.

She needed to increase the distance between them. He probably wouldn't allow much, but even a few feet might make the difference. How long had it been since Rick left? Five or ten minutes at most?

"So how long have you been doing work for the sheriff's office?"

"Just started." He was now watching her as closely as she watched him.

"Must be interesting—"

He wasn't listening to her. When he lowered the portfolio to the floor, adrenaline shot through her. Turning, she made it to the front door and ripped the dead bolt open. One second she was reaching for the doorknob and the next she had hit the ground with enough force that she lay stunned. She was still gasping when he grabbed her arms and dragged her backward.

Nooo! This couldn't be happening!

The edge of the first stair riser slammed into her spine. She screamed. As her feet grazed the bottom stair tread, she tried pushing off it. As long as she was on her back, she was at his mercy. If she could just get onto her feet, she at least had a fighting chance.

Somehow she got onto her knees, but she still couldn't get her feet into position. They were on the second floor now. She screamed and kept on screaming.

Another staircase. When they hit the top, he hefted her

body up as if she were a side of beef, locking his thick arm across her throat. Short, frantic gasps escaped her lips.

She raked his face with her nails and bucked, twisting, trying to break free as he continued to drag her backward. He tightened his hold, using his free hand to fling open a door.

And then they were outside. On some kind of roof deck and it was pouring rain.

"Let's see if you can fly."

Chapter Eight

Tuesday, 12:52 p.m.

Something was wrong.

Rick already had the car door open when the SUV slid to a stop at the curb. He'd tried calling Jillian twice on the house phone and then her cellular and gotten no answer. Racing for his front door, he tried the cell again. When she still didn't pick up this time, he punched in 911 and gave the address.

As he bounded up onto the porch, he was already thinking about the fact that he didn't have a weapon, that the only gun in the house was safely tucked beneath boxer shorts.

The first sign of a struggle was just inside the door. He stepped over the downed chair and kept moving, listening intently. He covered the lower floor in a matter of seconds, grabbing a knife on his way through the kitchen, and then headed for the front of the house again and hit the stairs.

Why was the house so damn silent? Because he was too late? Because he hadn't been paying close enough attention? Because after she'd survived everything else, he'd gotten Jillian killed?

At the top of the landing, he turned left, found his bedroom empty. Then he heard a thump overhead. On the third floor.

Tossing the knife onto the dresser, Rick grabbed the .45 automatic from the top drawer. The weapon felt almost foreign in his hand and at the same time uncomfortably familiar.

Back in the hall, he took the next set of stairs fast. As he hit the top of them, a stiff gust of wind roared through the roof deck's open doorway. He kept moving, his back pressed to the wall. Just short of the opening, he stopped. Shifting forward, he got his first look.

And didn't like it.

A man held a .38 snub-nosed revolver to Jillian's right temple. Jillian's eyes were closed as if she waited for the inevitable, and the arm locked across her throat kept her struggling to breathe.

Rick stepped outside where rain sliced the already heavy air, coming down harder, smacking the slate roof and pinging against lead gutters.

"You don't want to hurt her." As Rick advanced, the punk retreated, taking Jillian with him. Both men knew she was a bargaining chip. "If you do, you're never getting off this roof alive."

The punk thumbed back the hammer, but didn't say anything.

Desperate to defuse the situation, Rick immediately lowered his weapon, hoping to give the illusion that he wasn't an immediate threat.

"Maybe we should all stand down for a few minutes," Rick said. "Think about what's happening here."

"Shut up."

"Hurting her isn't going to give you what you want."

The punk lifted and rotated his wrist so that the end of the gun muzzle was pressed tightly to Jillian's scalp again. "I said shut up."

A combination of rage and fear twisted inside Rick, but he managed to control it.

"Jillian?" When she didn't react to her name, Rick tried again. "Jillian. You're going to be okay. You hear me? You just need to stay calm."

Jillian opened her eyes and looked at him. Her gaze was direct. After all that she'd been through, he'd expected to see terror in them, but what he saw was anger. Good. She wasn't done fighting, after all.

He returned his attention to the man holding her.

The whine of sirens could be heard now in the distance. They were probably still blocks away, but they were closing in fast.

"Maybe you should cut your losses," Rick suggested. "You haven't really hurt anyone yet. Let the girl go and you can probably get a pretty good deal. Maybe even a plea bargain with no time." He lied of course. When this was over, he'd make certain this scumbag landed behind bars.

Rick's hands tightened on the gun. He'd brought it back up several seconds ago, but the punk didn't seem to have noticed. The punk glanced down, maybe checking out the street. He would be feeling the pressure now. He knew he'd have to make a choice soon.

And he wasn't the only one being forced to make a decision here.

So far, Rick hadn't seen any indication that the guy might back down. Which meant Rick was going to have to make a move very shortly, too. The rain continued to mess with his vision. How badly would it affect his aim? The punk holding Jillian would be even worse off. With the glasses that he wore, it would be like looking through a rain-speckled windshield.

"Think about what you're doing," Rick said.

The punk didn't respond. The sirens suddenly went silent. Even from three stories below them and with the rain still pounding, the sound of car doors being slammed was distinct. As if drawn by them, the punk moved to look down again, taking Jillian with him. As he twisted to check out the street below this time, his hand shifted as it had before, the gun muzzle drifting marginally away from the side of her head.

Rick squeezed off the first round. It slammed into the punk's right shoulder, high and to the right. The impact drove him backward, the revolver muzzle rising and moving away from Jillian. But the scumbag still had her.

Closing in, Rick got off another shot. It tore into the upper arm. The man barely moved. What in the hell was keeping him on his feet? Given the amount of blood, he should be dead.

"Let her go!" Rick was almost there now. Unless the son of a bitch released Jillian, the next shot was going into his skull. The man groaned. The next thing Rick knew, Jillian was being dragged off the roof. The son of a bitch still hadn't let go of her. Screaming, she latched on to a section of railing.

Already lunging for her, Rick reached her right arm.
As his fingers closed around it, he was hauled forward.
Dropping his weapon, he grabbed her left wrist.

"Hang on!"

Jillian gasped, the arm across her throat choking her,
the man's weight threatening to take her down with
him. Her terrified eyes stared into Rick's. He cursed the
rain that made her skin unbelievably slick. No matter
how hard he squeezed, he could feel his hold slipping.

"I've got you, Jillian. I'm not going to let you fall.
You understand?" Rain blurred his vision. "I won't let
go. No matter what."

Rick gritted his teeth in pain. Between Jillian and the
man who still hung on to her, there must have been three
hundred pounds pulling at his arms. He yelled for help,
but even if the officers moved quickly, it was unlikely
they'd make the roof in time.

The man holding her was losing his grip. His legs
pumped faster, as if trying to climb air. With the baseball
cap gone, he looked younger, maybe only twenty-four
or twenty-five. As the cops below shouted out, the man
seemed to look over his shoulder. Then simply let go.

As his terrified scream plummeted, Jillian glanced
back.

"No, Jillian!" Rick yelled. "Don't look down! Keep
your eyes on me!"

For a panicked moment he thought he was going to lose
her, but then she turned back, her gaze connecting with
his.

"Good girl. Now let's get you up here with me."

Chapter Nine

Tuesday, 9:18 p.m.

Jillian stood in the bedroom doorway for several seconds as she tried to get her bearings. The living room of the penthouse condo belonging to a friend of Rick's was quiet and peaceful, giving the illusion of safety and normalcy. Something she had desperately needed after this afternoon.

She had been so exhausted when they'd arrived, she hadn't paid much attention to the layout or the decor. Instead she had showered and gone to bed. And since there didn't appear to be any interior lights on anywhere, she assumed that Rick had probably done the same, that he was asleep behind one of the closed doors.

She glanced down at the white oxford shirt Rick had lent her to sleep in, checking to be sure all the buttons were done up. What time was it, anyway? The middle of the night, or sometime earlier?

Moving cautiously among the furniture, she wandered toward the large wall of glass. But when she reached it, the view wasn't of Charleston as she'd expected, but of a lighted swimming pool shimmering like blue ice in the center of a large private patio. And just beyond, a full moon scaled the darkness. Instead of beautiful, the pool looked lonely in its isolation.

As lonely and isolated as she felt at the moment.

She tried to shut out the horrible images of the nightmare that had awakened her moments earlier, but the images of burned-out trucks, of unrecognizable bodies continued to play over and over again like a short-looped film.

Her hand crept up to her bruised throat, rested there almost in a protective measure. She'd nearly been dragged off the roof. Even now, just thinking about this afternoon left her shaky inside, and her emotions uncomfortably close to the surface.

Lowering her hand, she wrapped her arms in front of her. Rick had asked her to trust him. But how could she? As she stared out at the night, she rubbed her arms slowly. Trusting anyone—needing anyone—was something she had always found very difficult.

The sound of soft snoring broke the stillness.

Turning, she saw Rick stretched out on the couch, and was surprised that she hadn't seen him there sooner. For several seconds she just listened to the comforting sound, then moved across the room, sinking onto the large ottoman in front of him.

The tired warrior.

Reflected light from the pool flickered across his strong features. His nearly black hair was tousled as if he'd run his hand through it, and he still needed a shave.

Emotion tightened her chest. He'd risked his life for her, for someone he'd known less than a day. He'd said he wouldn't let go, and he hadn't. She owed him so damn much at this point.

His lips were slightly parted, his breath easing in and out rhythmically. She'd been fighting the attraction all day, but now that there was no one to witness it, no one to judge her for feeling things that she shouldn't, she gave up the struggle.

The white oxford shirt lay open, revealing a muscled chest that rose and fell, rose and fell. The button of his jeans had been undone, the zipper lowered by several seductive inches.

But when her gaze reached his feet, her insides did this funny little thing that made it nearly impossible to breathe. The right foot was bare, but the left one… The laces had been loosened, but the shoe remained, half on, half off.

Trust him? Maybe she already did, at least a little bit. Otherwise she wouldn't still be with him.

"Can't sleep?" His voice was low and slightly raspy.

Jillian straightened, instantly embarrassed. How long had he been awake? And then she realized that with her back to the room's only light source, he wouldn't have been able to see her face, anyway.

Jillian pretended to shrug the kinks out of her shoulders. "I came to see if you were hungry."

He didn't say anything for several seconds, during which she wondered if she'd been wrong about the lighting.

"Food sounds good." Sitting up, Rick rubbed his face. "There's a Chinese place not far from here. I could pick up some takeout."

Even though they were on the nineteenth floor and

in a building with twenty-four-hour security, she wasn't ready to be left alone. Even for a short while. "Is there food here?"

"Probably. Soup, maybe."

"I could throw something together," she said.

Reaching over, he turned on the table lamp, dispelling the sense of intimacy. "Sure. Why don't you relax while I catch a shower, and then we'll figure out something together?"

Maybe it was the light that did it, or maybe it was the nightmare catching up with her again. Either way, she couldn't sit still.

A few minutes later, having changed into jeans and a sweater, she found the wall switches just inside the kitchen door. The room was a pleasant surprise. Plenty of counter space, most of it black granite. Beautiful cherry cabinets with glass fronts. Two side-by-side refrigerators. When Rick had said his friend had been gone for nearly a week now and wouldn't be back for another three, she'd been worried that she'd be unable to find much in the way of makings. But in this cook's paradise, there was bound to be something.

After checking both refrigerators, she came up with milk that was one day short of expiration, eggs, bacon, cheese and some mushrooms that were still hanging in there. So if nothing else, there was the standard omelet. Opening the freezer, she found a package of frozen shrimp and in the pantry, grits.

Shrimp and grits. Like the omelet, suitable for breakfast, lunch or dinner. At least in the South. She couldn't recall the last time she'd had it, but it had been a staple of her young life.

She'd been nervous about returning to Charleston and confronting her past—a silly fear, perhaps, but still very real. When she'd left here, she'd been an emotionally lost child. That child still resided deep inside and always would, but for the first time in her life she was beginning to embrace her past. Because it had made her strong, a survivor, and she needed to be both those things right now. Not just for herself, but for Megan, too.

The bacon was nearly done and she was cleaning shrimp when Rick came up behind her. His hair was still damp and he'd exchanged the white shirt for a faded black T-shirt that stretched across his muscled chest.

"Smells great." He took the half-peeled shrimp from her fingers. "Not the shrimp. The bacon." He gave her a slight nudge with his shoulder. "I can finish these." He glanced over at her. "How are you doing?"

"Okay," she offered, her awareness of him escalating by the second. "My neck is sore and I have bruises in places I've never had them before, but I'll survive. What about you?" Several times after he'd pulled her onto the roof, she'd watched him wince as he tested his shoulders.

"I'm fine." He motioned to the bar stools at the end of the island. "Why don't you sit?"

"That's okay." Jillian crossed to the stove, where she stirred the grits.

She needed to stay busy. Keep her mind off…everything. She couldn't remember the exact moment when it had happened—when she'd stopped keeping time like a normal person. Now it was measured not in hours and minutes, but in the hours that Megan had been gone. Nearly twenty-one had passed with no real news.

No sightings.

Nothing to hang hope on.

After the real artist had completed the three sketches this afternoon, he'd placed them side by side on the conference table and asked her to check them over one last time. Was there anything she wanted him to change? Even at that point, looking at them had made her uncomfortable, but it was the possibility that she'd gotten them wrong that had really terrified her.

Three faces brought to life. But were they the right three?

What if she'd screwed up?

Jillian left the spoon in the pan of grits. "Shouldn't we have heard something by now? I mean, if the sketches were on the six-o'clock news…" Her hand shook as she skewered the last piece of bacon, draping it across several layers of paper towel.

She kept her back to Rick, afraid to let him see just how frightened she was.

"Tips have to be checked out," Rick said. "Which takes time." He handed her the shrimp and a glass of white wine.

She knew that he was right, but that didn't make it any easier. For Megan, for the other women, time was the enemy. And for Jillian, too. If something didn't happen pretty soon, she was going to go out of her mind. Only last week a boy who had been missing for more than four years had been found alive less than fifty miles from where he'd been kidnapped. How had his parents coped? How had they managed never to lose faith, when Jillian's faith was already so miserably weak?

She slipped the shrimp in with the sautéed onions. As she stirred them together, her hand was shaking again.

And what about Megan? What was her faith like right now? Was there even an ounce of hope left inside her?

"What if I got it wrong, though, and no one calls? What happens next?"

"By now, the lab is working on fingerprinting your car and looking for any trace evidence."

Rick found place mats and napkins and set two places at one end of the island. As she was giving everything a final stir, he left her alone in the kitchen for several minutes. Soft jazz suddenly filled the room. Glancing up, she spotted the small overhead speaker.

Rick refilled her wineglass.

As he handed it to her, the scents of shampoo and soap and male skin reached her. Taking the wine, Jillian realized she couldn't remember drinking the first one. Under normal circumstances, she wasn't much of a drinker—a glass of wine now and again. But maybe for tonight at least, she'd let it take the edge off.

Rick placed his glass next to one of the place mats. "I was just trying to narrow down the last time a woman fixed shrimp and grits for me."

"And have you?"

"Janey Burnham," he said, and seemed to spend several seconds recalling her attributes.

Naturally, Jillian was curious about what those might be, but she wasn't going to ask. "Fiancée?"

"Almost." He shook his head and, offering up a quick grin, downed half his own wine. "I was ready to pop the question. She was damned pretty. Had legs that—"

"But you didn't?"

"No. She'd brought over shrimp and grits that night. I put on some soft music, opened up a bottle of fizzy." He lifted his glass for emphasis. "The ring, which was the best I could afford at the time, was tucked into my pocket. I had high hopes and things were going really well. Or at least I thought they were until I took my first bite."

This was a side of him that she hadn't seen. She knew what he was doing. Trying to distract her. And why not let him believe that it was working?

"What happened?"

"She'd forgotten to peel the shrimp."

"So you didn't ask her to marry you because of that?"

"How could I?" He downed the rest of the wine. "But I did take her to the eighth-grade dance that year."

Maybe if she hadn't been so distracted by everything else, she would have seen the punch line coming.

Jillian smiled and handed Rick the large serving bowl. "Well, I'm not looking for a ring or even a dance, so try not to be too judgmental here tonight. Okay?"

After his first bite, Rick glanced up. "Now, if Janey's had tasted like this, we'd probably have a dozen kids by now."

"Have you ever been married?" On the ride back last night she'd asked if he was married. His simple no answer hadn't excluded the possibility that he was divorced. Or that he was currently in a relationship.

He nodded. "Once." He reached for the serving dish. "How about you? Ever take the plunge?"

"No. Never even been close." She watched him scrape out another plateful. "Your father was a cop. Was that why you became one?"

"His father was a cop, too. And I had grown up around law enforcement types, so it seemed like the natural flow."

"Were they upset you left to do what you're doing now?"

"Death-penalty cases, you mean?" He shrugged. "Somebody's got to do it."

Not a real answer, but a cocktail-party response. She glanced down at her dinner. More than half of it remained, but there was no way she could eat it. What about Megan? When was it that Megan had eaten last? Twenty-four hours ago when they'd stopped for dinner? Megan had barely eaten anything then, said she wasn't overly hungry. What if that was her last meal?

Last meal…

Jillian couldn't get off the stool fast enough. "I can't…"

He caught up to her in the hallway just outside her bedroom door, grabbing her from behind and turning her into him. His arms closed around her, locking her to his hard body, trapping her hands between them.

"You can't *what,* Jillian?"

She clenched her eyes. "I can't stop thinking about what's happening to her. Is she being raped right now? As I sit here eating a meal in safety. Is she wondering where I am? Why no one has rescued her? Or is she already dead?" Jillian pushed with her lower arms, but he wouldn't let her go.

"Stop doing this to yourself."

If only she could. "I can't stop thinking about the sketches. What if they aren't right? What if it's the only thing that can bring her home and I screwed them up? If I'm the reason that—"

This time he was the one who pushed. She found herself trapped between the wall and Rick. He pressed his forehead to hers, forcing her to meet his gaze. His fingers spread, their tips gently brushing her cheeks, his thumbs settling just below her jawline.

"You're the reason she's going to make it. The only reason. Because you fought back. And it's not just your sister's life that will be saved, it's the lives of the other women in that truck. And of the women who won't be kidnapped in the future because of you, Jillian."

For several seconds they just stared at each other. She could feel her pulse kicking against the pads of his thumbs, and she couldn't escape the jackhammering of his heart beneath her palms.

They were both breathing a little too hard and a little too fast to pretend that what was happening here wasn't happening. She was aware of him in ways that she hadn't been aware of a man in a long time. In ways that she didn't want to be aware of him.

Her breathing turned suddenly shallow, as if they'd burned up all the air between them. Slowly he lowered his mouth, angling hers up to his. She wasn't sure which of them actually groaned as their lips met, but the sound went through her, settling at her very core.

His mouth claimed hers as his hand drifted downward, wrapping around her waist, pulling her closer still.

She shouldn't be doing this but couldn't recall why. Was it wrong to feel safe? To feel something besides fear? To touch? To be touched?

A warning bell was going off in her head. She tried to ignore it. And then she realized it wasn't in her head, at all.

The door.

As the door buzzer sounded again, Rick pulled back, and then, without saying anything, turned and walked away.

Jillian sagged against the wall. Their bodies no longer touched, but she could still feel him. She could still taste him. What in the hell had she been thinking?

She hadn't been. Because that's what she'd wanted. To forget for a few minutes.

But how was she going to forget what had just happened?

Chapter Ten

Rick checked the small security monitor in the foyer. Nate Langley stared into the camera, his features somewhat distorted by the wide-angle lens.

Rick glanced toward the hallway where he'd left Jillian. It was a damn kiss. Nothing more. Maybe he shouldn't have done it, but they were all adults here. After an additional few seconds of cooling off, Rick opened the door.

"Hope you don't mind my just stopping by, but I was in the neighborhood."

"Come on in." Rick stepped back, quickly assessing the man. Gone was the polished exterior of even twenty-four hours ago. The detective looked like a man who probably hadn't slept in more than thirty-six hours, and possibly couldn't recall the last time he'd eaten. Or been completely dry.

Glancing down, Rick saw the paper bag Langley carried in his left hand. He didn't actually believe Langley had been in the area, and because good news usually came by way of a phone call, and bad news in person, Rick suspected they were about to get the latter.

But how bad? Had the truck been found empty? Or like eight years ago, had it been found burned, all the victims dead?

Either one was going to send Jillian over the edge. Unfortunately, there was no way he could shield her from the pain. Nor would she want him to. He still didn't know her very well, but he knew that much. Jillian didn't try to avoid the hard stuff, no matter how bad it got.

But even if Rick couldn't protect Jillian from the news, perhaps he could find some way to soften it, at least. And for that reason, Rick led Langley toward the kitchen, where they would have slightly more privacy.

He expected them to have the space to themselves, but instead of retreating to the bedroom as he'd expected, Jillian was already at the stove, cleaning up.

He could see the tension in her shoulders. As much as he didn't want to be aware of her, he was. Of the way her black jeans cupped her firm backside. The way the black sweater hugged her breasts. The way her dark ponytail swayed as she moved.

It was his turn to consider retreating. To the living room. But before he could turn, Jillian greeted Langley. "Hello, Detective."

The two of them had resolved their differences to a certain extent—mostly because Langley had rejected Durwood's theory where Jillian was concerned. But Jillian would still know that Langley's appearance here tonight wasn't a social call.

When Rick tried to catch her gaze, she avoided meeting his eyes.

Langley placed the sack on the counter next to her. "It's the contents of your and Megan's purses. I know you've probably reported most of the credit cards stolen, but I figured the driver's license would come in handy."

She nodded. "Thanks."

Was that the reason for Langley's visit, then? To bring personal effects? It still seemed like a long reach. Especially when he could have sent anyone by with them.

Moving to the counter, Langley glanced at Jillian's plate as he pushed it away. "Looks good." At five-nine, he was forced to hike himself onto the barstool.

Instead of sitting, Rick chose to lean against the counter, mostly because it allowed him to keep an eye on Jillian. She had yet to look in his direction, though.

Jillian placed the pan in the sink. "Would you like an omelet, Detective? I'd be happy to make one for you."

Langley actually looked tempted for a few seconds. "No, thanks. This needs to be quick." He leaned forward, resting his elbows on the granite surface. "Your hunch paid off, Brady. Five minutes after the sketches were broadcast, we got a call. The name of the woman Jillian and her sister stopped to help is Debra Wert. She works for Miramar Cruises out of Miami, calling on travel agencies in Florida, Georgia and South Carolina."

Jillian had been rinsing out a sponge, but now let it fall into the sink. "Someone recognized her based on the drawing?"

Langley nodded. "We did a comparison to her

Florida driver's license and I'd say you did a remarkable job."

Jillian took a deep breath. "What about the other two sketches? Anything on them?"

"Nothing so far. All three aired locally, but we weren't in time to make the national news at six-thirty. Most of the Web pages of the major networks have it up now, though, and Fox and CNN are running it, so we may get something from one of them."

Her fingers shook almost imperceptibly as she picked up the sponge again. "Then maybe we'll hear something after the eleven-o'clock news."

Rick shook his head. "It may not happen that fast. There's a difference between a victim and a suspect, Jillian. People are always quicker to come forward to identify a victim."

Langley agreed. "IDing a suspect is riskier to the individual reporting it. And because it is, it's not unusual for it to take more time for the calls to start coming in."

Rick couldn't read Jillian's reaction. She was so damn good at hiding her emotions most of the time. Which was probably just as well. Because whenever she didn't, she somehow ended up in his arms.

When he glanced toward Langley again, the detective was watching him watch Jillian.

"So who did the actual ID of the Wert woman?" Rick asked.

"A Charleston customer. He had an appointment scheduled with her for Monday, but she didn't show."

"Have you contacted Miramar for her itinerary?" Rick asked. "Checked to see where else she was supposed to be?"

Frowning, Langley pulled the nearly empty serving bowl closer, as if it were a bowl of peanuts left out for company. "I've been known to be competent." He scooped out a shrimp with his fingers and he popped it into his mouth. "She makes her own schedule. At the end of each week, she turns in her appointment log. Last week's report was postmarked on Saturday from Vero Beach where she lives." Langley pulled the serving bowl of shrimp and grits even closer and grabbed the serving spoon.

Rick poured wine in a fresh glass and placed it in front of the detective. "What about using her credit card account to narrow down the possible location of her abduction."

Langley eyed him, then relented and lifted the glass. "In the works." Having finished off the serving bowl, he glanced at Jillian's plate, but didn't make a move on it. "Durwood is checking federal databases. Maybe something will turn up there."

Rick settled against the counter again. "Have you given any thought to the possibility that there might be a law enforcement connection?"

Langley frowned. "Go on."

"Eight years ago the only witness suddenly died as she was being brought out of a medically induced coma. And then today, how did they find Jillian so quickly? How did they know she was staying with me? It wasn't as if it had been advertised."

"I read Jane Doe's report from eight years ago. She was in pretty bad shape when she came out of that truck. The doctors thought it unlikely that she'd make it, or that, if she did survive, she'd ever be able to communicate." Langley wiped his face tiredly. "As for what happened today, they could have been watching the sheriff's office. Tracked you from there."

"We weren't followed. I checked. And that still doesn't explain how they knew a police artist was coming to my house and at what time he was expected." Rick ran a hand through his hair. He would have preferred to discuss most of this where Jillian wouldn't have to hear it, but that obviously wasn't an option. "What about the scene log? My name appears on it. Any possibility someone got a look at it?" They both knew that there was.

"Okay." Langley held up his hands. "I'll check everyone at the scene last night and anyone who had access to the log against a list of those involved in the Midnight Run case." He lowered his arms. "But for the record, I think you're wrong."

"What about going a step further and adding a list of anyone involved in the investigation of my father's death, too?"

Langley let out a sharp sigh. "Sure. At least that list will be a much shorter one." Langley slipped his hand into his pocket. "There was another reason that I wanted to stop by. We have a name for Jillian's attacker. Randy Gardner. Small-time hood with a drug problem. He's also a suspect in three recent arson cases." Langley passed Rick the plastic evidence bag containing a small blue notebook. "Recognize it?"

Rick nodded. "Yes. It's my father's. Where did you find it?"

"In Randy Gardner's pocket. Unfortunately the last eighteen pages have been ripped out."

Rick turned it over in his hand, wished he could open

it. How many times had he seen his dad slipping it in or out of a pocket? Or flipping through it, rereading the notes he'd made?

"Do you think he killed your father?"

Rick looked up with a frown. "Gardner? No. He may have been there when it happened, but I don't buy him as my father's killer. He found it difficult handling an unarmed woman. There's no way that he could have disarmed my father and used the weapon to kill him."

Langley wiped his mouth with the napkin in front of him. "Too bad you had to go and shoot our best lead."

Rick knew what Langley was getting at. If Randy Gardner was alive, they'd have their first big break in both cases. The same person who had hired Gardner to kill Jillian had probably also paid for his father's murder.

Rick frowned. "You said that Gardner was tied to several recent arsons? Any possibility that the properties were owned by the same person? That maybe he hired Gardner to burn a few buildings and then decided to give him a promotion?"

"From what we have so far, it doesn't appear as if Randy was hired to torch any of them. It looks as if he just liked to watch things burn."

Langley sat back. If anything, he looked even more exhausted than when he'd arrived. He used two hands to scrub his face this time. Then he climbed off the stool. "I'll let you know if anything else comes up."

"Thanks for coming," Rick said.

Langley held out his hand. "I need that notebook back, by the way. It's the evidence I need to have your father's case reopened."

Time unknown

MEGAN'S BACK COLLIDED with the wall. Jolted from one nightmare into another, she tried to focus on her surroundings. Something was different. The truck was no longer moving.

She glanced up at the roof. The last time she'd been awake, sunlight had shone through a random series of one-inch holes. There was no light now, so it must be night again. But was it 7:00 p.m. or 5:00 a.m.?

And did it really matter in this hellhole where she and the others were trapped? She had no idea where they were. Cops probably didn't, either. But did that mean Jilly hadn't made it? That she was dead?

Megan's chest tightened with sorrow and pain as she struggled to hold off the insidious terror that lurked below the surface, the horror that sucked every ounce of will out of her.

If her sister hadn't made it, no one was ever going to come for her.

Megan shivered, for the first time realizing how cold she was. The temperature inside the truck had dropped ten or twenty degrees. As best she could tell, the truck's lack of movement hadn't fazed the other women. Slowly she'd begun to realize that for some reason she wasn't being given the same amount of drugs as the others. Why? Being singled out wasn't a good thing. She swallowed a sob, not wanting to think about what it might mean.

One of the cab doors opened, slammed shut. Several seconds later the sound repeated. By the time the back door of the truck rolled up, Megan had wedged herself into the corner again to wait. To fear.

The taller man—the one with red hair and who usually carried a shotgun—climbed into the back of the truck. He turned on the light as he did every time, but when he pulled out a set of keys, she knew something was different about this stop.

After unlocking her manacles, he hauled her out of the straw. Her teeth chattered now, and as she started to sway on her feet, she realized how weak she was, how stiff and unresponsive her leg muscles had become.

"You say anything, you try to talk to anyone, I'll kill you." He pulled back his leather coat. A large pistol was shoved into his waistband. "Then I'll kill them."

The man passed her off to his partner who waited just outside. Even before her feet touched the ground, he'd grabbed her wrist.

Did he actually expect her to run? And then she wondered if she should. Either she'd get lucky—would manage to outrun them despite the fact that she hadn't eaten in at least twenty-four hours, that fear and cold temperatures had robbed her of every bit of her energy resources—or she'd be dead. In a matter of seconds she wouldn't have to fear anything ever again.

But even as she contemplated giving up, Megan also thought about her sister. As long as Megan had reason to believe her sister might still be alive, she owed it to Jillian to stay that way, too.

Megan checked her surroundings. They'd pulled off onto some kind of paved access road, she realized, and into a dense stand of pine trees. Small islands of unmelted snow floated out from the deeper shade. They had traveled north, but it could have been West Viginia, or even Canada.

All she knew was that a frigid breeze cut through her and, in the distance, she could hear traffic. But how close? On a cold, cloudless night, sound could travel for miles and miles.

The man restraining her held a sack in his other hand and she wondered what was in it. In most ways, he looked fairly normal, certainly not like the monster he was.

"Where are we?" she asked, figuring the worst he could do was not answer. Which is exactly what he did.

The tall one hopped down and lowered the door. "Did you check it out?"

"There's one car in the lot, but I didn't see nobody, and the hood's iced up. It's been there a few hours."

"Did you make the call?"

"Yeah. He's got the cash and he'll phone in thirty minutes with directions."

"Good. Without any holdups we should make New Carlyle by noon."

Chapter Eleven

Jillian had stepped out of the shower, was staring out the large window over the jetted tub. When she'd gone to bed last night, a million lights had sparkled in the distance, but with dawn only hours away, there were far fewer of them now.

She hadn't slept well. Caffeine would probably help the headache, but not much else. She kept going back over everything in her head. The kiss. What Langley had said in the kitchen last night about Rick shooting their best lead. Until that moment she hadn't fully recognized what saving her life had cost both of them—the identity of his father's killer and maybe her sister's life.

Her cell phone rang. Grabbing a towel, she raced to the bedroom to answer it.

"I'm not sure if I'm doing the right thing here." The woman's unfamiliar voice sounded nervous and uncertain. "But I stopped in a rest area a few minutes ago, and, I…I don't know. Maybe this is some kind of joke. If it is, I'm sorry, but…"

"No—please!" Jillian's adrenaline spiked. "Talk to me."

"Well, there's this message on the back of the stall door in the ladies' room."

Jillian barely managed to get the towel wrapped around her before Rick was knocking at the bedroom door. She opened it, motioned him in. "What kind of message? Where's the rest area?"

Her gaze rose to Rick's. He was watching her face intently.

"Just outside Blue Summit. In West Virginia."

"What's…what's the message?" Jillian couldn't keep her voice steady.

"Just this number. And the words *new car.*" She broke off briefly. "It looks as if… I don't know how else to say this. I think it's been written with blood."

Jillian's heart stopped dead and it took her several seconds to recover, to be able to string words together again. "Please call 911. No one can go into that bathroom."

"I can't stand guard," the woman said, suddenly sounding even more nervous.

"My sister was kidnapped. She left that message. It's all we have right now." Jillian could hear the desperation in her own voice. "You have to make sure no one goes in there."

When Rick motioned for her to give him the phone, Jillian realized she had been shouting.

"I'm sorry." She needed to keep the woman on the phone. "I'm going to put a friend of mine on. Please tell him everything."

As soon as he took it, Jillian scooped up jeans and sweater and dived back into the bathroom. Tossing down the towel, she jerked on her clothes. Her hands were shaking. Everything inside her was shaking. She grabbed a brush, ripped it through her hair in fast strokes, then tossed her hair, still wet, over her shoulders.

For the first time in hours Jillian allowed herself to hope.

When she opened the door into the bedroom, the room was empty. Jillian grabbed her meager belongings, stuffing them and her few toiletries into a plastic bag. She had to get to West Virginia, fast.

Megan.

As Jillian kicked her way into her shoes, Rick reappeared in the doorway, looking equally tense, his brows drawn down over his dark eyes.

"I've contacted Durwood and Langley. We'll call airlines from the car."

Wednesday, 9:32 a.m.

WITH NO LUGGAGE to pick up, when the plane landed in Roanoke, Virginia, at 8:28, they'd gone straight to the car-rental counter. Ten minutes later they'd been on the road, heading southwest toward Blue Summit, West Virginia.

He'd gotten a call from Langley just before they'd boarded. The investigation into the death of Rick's father had been officially reopened.

As happy as he was about the news, he recognized that it wasn't his only objective now. As much as Rick wanted to catch his father's killer, as much as his father would have wanted his name cleared, Jim Brady would want something else even more—the men responsible for the Midnight Run Murders. Bringing them to justice had been what he'd devoted the last months and days of his life to. What he'd given his last breath for.

And what Rick was going to finish for his dad. He was going to find justice for the victims of eight years ago, and even if it was the last thing he did, he was going to make sure that Jillian's sister and the other women were rescued.

He didn't fool himself into believing Durwood was going to be happy to see him or Jillian. And most likely, the special agent was going to be damned pissed when they showed up at the rest area. Not that Rick or anyone else could have kept Jillian away.

New car.

If Megan's message was right, they needed to be looking for another type of vehicle. Which would complicate the investigation.

Still twenty or thirty minutes from their destination, Rick looked over at Jillian. She hadn't pulled her hair back this morning. He liked it down. It softened her features some. Because the flight had been full, they hadn't been able to sit together, but sometime while they'd been in the air, she'd managed to put on makeup, partially concealing the dark shadows beneath her eyes and disguising the worst of the bruising from Gardner's attack. Recalling the moment on the roof and how differently it could have ended, Rick's pulse accelerated.

But it hadn't...

Rick pushed a hand through his hair. He needed to stay focused here. Needed to remember that no matter how desirable he found Jillian, the only reason they were together right now was that they wanted the same thing.

She'd been pretty quiet so far, hadn't said much since

they'd left Roanoke. He wondered if it was strictly that she was worried about her sister, or if she was thinking about the coming confrontation with Durwood. They hadn't exactly hit it off. Durwood's fault, of course.

Rick glanced out the window. Heavy, dark clouds smothered the horizon and leached the color out of the late-November landscape. Melted snow bordered the road, and from the looks of it, they could get more at any time. His gaze lowered to the dashboard display. The current outside temperature had dropped in the past hour and now was thirty-two degrees. Neither of them was really dressed for the current weather.

Jillian shivered, rubbing her arms slowly as she stared at the road ahead.

Rick turned the heater up. "We'll get some heavier coats and gloves the first chance we get." They both wore lightweight leather coats meant for southern winters.

She folded the map away, tucked it overhead behind the visor. "Do you think that they'll be able to tell when she was there?"

"I don't know," Rick answered truthfully. "Maybe the best they'll be able to do is come up with a window of time. Then they can start searching for witnesses, anyone who might have seen her."

But it was something. At least it was a direction. And another crime scene meant the possibility of more information. But Megan's note also gave false hope to Jillian. Finding these bastards was still a long shot. Especially in the short term. And for Jillian, for her sister and the other women in the back of that truck, the short term was all that mattered.

He rubbed his face, wishing he didn't know the statistics on the number of women who simply vanished each year, and that, once taken, those victims usually lasted only a few short years.

"It should be coming up soon," Jillian said, her voice suddenly more tense than the last time she'd spoken. She wasn't just preparing herself for the coming confrontation with Durwood, but also to come face-to-face with the message her sister had left them. Possibly written in blood.

He couldn't imagine the torment Jillian must be coping with right now. She'd been through so much during the past thirty-six hours, more than most people had to deal with in a lifetime. What had she been like before her life had turned into this nightmare?

Last night he'd thought that he'd seen hints of that woman, of the soft, vulnerable core beneath that tough exterior of hers. Their kiss haunted him. And now he couldn't forget the sight of her standing in the middle of the bedroom this morning, the towel barely covering her warm, damp skin. He couldn't recall the last time he'd wanted to take a woman to bed quite as much as he did Jillian.

"There," Jillian said, pointing at the rest-area sign.

Two more miles and he saw the rest area off to the right. A line of fir trees partially obscured the compound of green concrete-block buildings sitting at the top of a sharp incline. Because barricades blocked the entrance road, Rick pulled in behind a line of marked and unmarked law-enforcement vehicles. He was doing a lot of that the past few days. And he was beginning to realize that there were aspects of police work that he missed.

Maybe his father was right. Once a cop, always a cop.

For a brief second before they climbed out, their gazes met. He wanted to remind her not to get her expectations up, that a note left in a bathroom wasn't necessarily going to bring Megan home, but he didn't. If the call this morning had allowed her to scrape up even a little hope, he didn't want to be the one to take it away. Let her cling to it for as long as she could.

"Ready?"

Nodding, she reached for the door handle.

They could have taken the long route and stayed on pavement, but when Jillian chose the most direct one, up the embankment, Rick followed.

He found it difficult to keep his eyes off her backside as she scrambled ahead of him.

A wet, heavy snow floated down, settling in Jillian's hair and making the hard-frozen ground tricky. Between the climb and the cold, by the time they reached the parking lot, Jillian's cheeks showed the first bit of color that he'd seen since meeting her.

The buildings were set up like most rest areas. Men's room on one side, the women's on the other, a covered, dimly lit breezeway in between with vending machines.

As soon as they stepped into the connecting breezeway, Durwood intercepted them, wearing a camel coat, heavy leather gloves and a frown. Jillian tried to duck into the restroom entrance, but Durwood caught her. "Can't go in yet. They're still processing. Shouldn't be but a few minutes more."

For a moment Rick thought he was going to have to intervene, but then Jillian backed off. He'd have to talk with her. This lead, this break in the investigation, had come directly to them, but it was unlikely that the next one would. Durwood was under no obligation to keep Jillian up-to-date with developments as they broke. So unless they wanted to be stuck sitting by the phone, waiting for news, Jillian was going to have to learn not to push quite so hard.

"Anything so far?" Rick asked.

"A set of clothes in the trash that might be Megan's." Durwood looked at Jillian. "If you're up to it, we're going to need you to ID them in a few minutes."

Jillian offered a slight nod, then immediately glanced away for several seconds, her hands inside her pockets. Rick's were in his pockets, too, but that was to keep himself from reaching out, offering comfort that she wouldn't accept.

Instead of protecting them from the wind, the wide hall seemed to funnel it right at them. Noticing the way Jillian hunched her shoulders against the cold, Rick moved just enough to shield her from the worst of it. "What about fingerprints?"

Durwood cleared his throat. "We picked up about thirty sets from the interior and exterior of the stall, the trash can and the faucet handles."

"Any leads on the type of vehicle they might be using now?" Rick asked.

"No. We may also have to consider the possibility that they have split up."

Jillian frowned. "So you're saying that there might not be just one car, but two?"

"Yes," Durwood answered. For the first time Rick saw pity in Durwood's eyes. "And we also have to consider the possibility that once their composites aired, they turned over the transporting of the women to another team."

Rick knew what Durwood was leaving unsaid. That there was one more scenario that was even worse than any of the ones he'd just posed. There was always the possibility that the kidnappers would do what they had done eight years ago. Only this time, Rick would bet, there wouldn't be any survivors left to talk.

As he'd told Jillian that first night. You don't get to choose. You just get to cope. But could anyone, no matter how tough they seemed emotionally, really cope with that kind of outcome? Even someone as strong as Jillian?

Rick glanced toward the restroom entrance. The voices of the officers inside echoed, but remained indistinguishable.

"What about blood evidence?" Rick asked.

Durwood pulled a throat lozenge out of his coat pocket. "There's blood on the clothes, on the door where the message was left and several smudges near the exit. We think she used a sharp edge on the tissue dispenser to cut herself. There's quite a bit of blood in that area. We also think that it was intentional. If that's the case, it could mean that she's still thinking clearly in spite of the drugs. That, given another opportunity, she might be able to give us something else, or possibly get away."

Jillian shifted forward, the action forcing Durwood's gaze in her direction. "How much blood?"

"A cut. The amount of blood doesn't suggest anything more."

Exhaling, Jillian nodded. Her gaze met Rick's briefly but almost immediately slipped away. Even in the dim lighting, he saw the panic in her eyes.

Durwood's willingness to answer questions surprised Rick. Perhaps Durwood was trying to make amends for being such an ass yesterday morning. The man owed Jillian a damn apology. And at some point Rick would make sure the federal agent gave her one. But for now, keeping the lines of communication open and friendly was more important to all of them.

"Any chance some of the blood could belong to one of the kidnappers?" Rick asked.

"It appears unlikely, but of course we'll know more when we have lab results."

Rick ran a hand through his hair. Hell. Every time they turned around, every time they seemed to get a break, it turned out not to be quite as good as they first thought. They knew Megan had been here. But what kind of vehicle had she been in?

"What about a time frame?" Rick asked. "Any way to pinpoint it? Even within a twelve-hour period?"

"We checked with the man who was on duty up until midnight. He says the trash can was emptied around eleven. So sometime after that."

"What about after midnight? Was anyone on duty?"

Durwood cleared his throat again. "We had a hard time getting hold of the worker assigned the midnight-to-eight shift, but McDaniel is on his way now to pick him up. They should be here shortly."

Two crime-scene techs walked out of the restroom, sharing the weight of a gray plastic tub. The one in front was a woman, short, in her twenties, dark hair, slightly heavyset; the other was a man of a similar height and in his thirties. Both wore baseball caps, sweatshirts, jeans and latex gloves.

"It's all yours, Special Agent Durwood," the female crime-scene tech said. "We still have the vending machines to print, but we're done in there."

"Thanks. I need to see the clothes you bagged for a few minutes."

The woman opened the tub and pulled out a rather large clear plastic bag that she handed to Durwood, who in turn passed it to Jillian.

Jillian's fingers were shaking as she took it. She held it for several seconds, just staring at it.

"You can't open it," Durwood cautioned. "If the clothes are hers, then they'll need to be checked for hair, fibers and DNA that might belong to the kidnappers."

She turned the bag over in her hands, and as she did, silent tears started to flow down her cheeks. "They're Megan's." After handing them back, Jillian turned and walked several feet away.

As Durwood gave the clothes to the tech, Rick's gaze followed Jillian. She was trying to pull it together as she always did.

Rick's chest tightened in anger and frustration. "What about the truck they were using originally? If we can locate it, it might give us a shot at identifying the vehicle or vehicles that we need to be looking for now."

"Every local law enforcement is doing their part, checking out their jurisdictions for an abandoned truck, flashing around the composites of the suspects. But just because she left her message here, doesn't mean that the change in vehicles didn't happen twenty minutes after Jillian escaped."

Durwood glanced over at the crime-scene techs finger-printing the soda machine, then swung his gaze back to

Rick. "For the past thirty-six hours, what we thought was our best lead could have been our worst one. Getting the sketches done sooner might have helped. Or maybe not. You were in law enforcement, Brady. You know what it's like. You get up in the morning, thinking it's going to be a good day, that the investigation you're working is coming together pretty well, and then you get a phone call and you're back to square one. Maybe we're not at square one, but we aren't that far from it, either."

Durwood paused again, this time to suck on the lozenge for several long seconds. "You'll have to excuse me, I've been fighting a sore throat." He used his tongue to shift the lozenge between his teeth and the inside of his right cheek. "I'm curious. Why did you leave law enforcement? You seem to have a knack for it."

Rick shoved his hands deeper into his pockets. "It was time to move on."

Durwood's gaze stayed on Rick's face for several seconds, then swung to the parking lot where McDaniel and another man walked toward them. "This is Mickey Smart," McDaniel said. "He was on duty last night."

Mickey Smart looked to be somewhere in his early forties. He was short and lanky. The maroon fleece jacket wasn't heavy enough for the weather. His jeans bunched at the bottom of his legs like a dancer's leg warmers.

From the way Mickey's hand shook and his complexion, Rick suspected that Mickey was one bottle away from a liver transplant, and even if he had been here, he'd probably been sleeping it off somewhere.

Durwood motioned at the entrance to the women's restroom. "Why don't we step on in there? At least we'll be out of the wind."

Concerned about Jillian, Rick hung back as Durwood, McDaniel and Smart walked ahead, stopping her when she would have followed. "Are you sure that you want to do this? See your sister's blood? I could take you back to the car." Rick released her. "I don't imagine we're going to learn anything new from Mickey."

Jillian took a deep breath and then let it out slowly. "I'm not going to wait in cars or motel rooms. I need to be doing something. Besides, I owe this to Megan."

Rick couldn't help but think that if Megan loved her sister, she wouldn't mind if Jillian wasn't there to see some of the hard stuff. And seeing blood, knowing that it belonged to someone you loved, that was the hardest of all.

But despite his reservations Rick held the door open for her. Her posture was even more erect than usual as she walked past him. It seemed that Mickey wasn't the only one who looked as if they were being asked to stand before a firing squad.

The room was divided into two areas. One held a row of sinks and a baby-changing table, the other the stalls. Everything but the concrete floor was painted the same putrid green as the exterior of the building. Four large fluorescent fixtures mounted to the high ceiling barely illuminated the space. On a sunny day the high windows would have helped some.

"You came on at midnight last night?" Durwood was asking when Jillian and Rick arrived.

"More like twelve-twenty." Shifting his weight from one foot to the other, Mickey scooped his too-long dirty-blond hair out of his eyes. "I was a little late."

"Did you see anything when you arrived?" Durwood asked.

"No." Mickey glanced down at his feet.

Jillian was no longer focused on Mickey Smart or the two federal agents. Her gaze was now taking in the room, stopping for a longer period at the trash can where the clothes would have been found and at the middle stall door that was barely visible from their current position. No doubt she had made the same assumption he had— that because of the amount of fingerprint powder covering it, the stall was the one her sister had used.

How did Jillian stand it?

Rick recalled the night of his father's murder. He'd gone out to where it had happened. His father's body had been taken away, but the scene was still being processed. They'd tried to keep him out, but of course they couldn't. Just as he hadn't been able to keep Jillian out. And at some point she'd insist on seeing the inside of the stall, and he wouldn't be able to stop her from doing that, either.

Was it bravery, though, or a form of self-torture?

"So you came in at twelve-twenty and left at eight," Durwood asked Mickey.

Mickey looked everywhere but at the special agent. "I wasn't feeling well. I went home around five."

"But you were here between twelve-twenty and five?" As Langley clarified the time, he pulled several sheets of tri-folded papers from the inside breast pocket of his coat.

"Yes, sir." Mickey nodded.

"I'd like you to take a look at several composites." Durwood showed him the two composite sketches and the enlargements of Megan's and Debra Wert's driver's license photos. "Did you see any of these people during that time?"

Mickey stared at each in turn. "I don't think so. But I'm not much good with faces."

Durwood looked as if he'd lost patience. "Mr. Smart, there couldn't have been that many people coming through here after midnight." Durwood handed each to Mickey again in turn. "I want you to look very closely. Maybe they had done something to alter their appearance some. A pair of glasses. A hat pulled low. A collar turned up."

Mickey studied the photos of the women the longest. Was that because, like most men, he noticed women more than he did men and thought he was more likely to recall their faces?

"No, sir." Mickey handed the last of them back. "I didn't see none of them."

When Jillian wandered toward the exit door, Rick hoped that she planned to step outside, because things were about to get ugly. Someone was lying. Either the worker on the four-to-midnight shift had lied about the time the trash was emptied, or Mickey was lying about the time he'd been on duty.

Jillian called Rick over to where she stood in front of the cleaning schedule posted on the back of the entrance door.

Rick's gaze followed her finger to the column. The initials for the person who came on at midnight were C.P, not M.S. Jillian had just discovered the reason Mickey was so damn nervous.

"Durwood?" Rick pointed to the schedule. "I believe the reason that Mickey is having such a hard time recognizing anyone is that he's lying to a federal agent and he stupidly believes he can get away with it."

Durwood took one look at the initials and then turned on his heels. "Mr. Smart, either you give me the truth right now, or I'm charging you with obstruction of justice. Now, who worked the midnight shift last night?"

"Cory." Mickey looked down at the floor. It wasn't just his hand shaking this time when he ran his fingers through his hair. Even his shoulders twitched. "Cory Prescott. He covered for me last night. I was sick, man. I didn't want to lose my job. And he owed me one."

Jillian pushed past Rick before he could stop her. She slapped Mickey hard across the cheek, would have done it again if Rick hadn't pulled her off.

Even as Rick pushed her backward, separating her from Mickey, she continued to scream, the strident sound echoing. "I don't give a damn about your job. I don't care if you get fired. I don't care if you can't find another job. There are seven women facing the worst kind of hell. You sick bastard!"

Durwood motioned to McDaniel. "Go get Cory Prescott. I'll take care of Mr. Smart here." Durwood grabbed him by the jacket and led him toward the exit. "You're an oxymoron, Mr. Smart. You know what that means?"

"No," he answered hesitantly.

"That means I'm going to have one of my men start some paperwork on you."

Chapter Twelve

Wednesday, 10:13 a.m.

Eyes clenched closed, Jillian leaned against the bathroom wall, her heart pounding, her lungs working double time. She'd lost it. She had just lost it.

And she needed to keep it together. Now more than ever. But how?

She heard the soft *slish* of a shoe brushing the grit on the concrete floor. She hadn't heard Rick come back, but, opening her eyes, she met his gaze.

"Maybe this is a good time to get some fresh air," he suggested. "They're done with the vending machines. We could grab some coffee and try to keep our asses from freezing off by sitting in the car until McDaniel shows up with Prescott."

She knew what he was trying to do. Give her an out. Let her walk away without confronting her sister's blood-written message.

Without answering him, Jillian pushed away from the wall, strode to the door of the middle stall. Fingerprint powder smudged much of it, especially around the handle.

Rick followed her, but kept silent.

Jillian took a deep breath, let it out slowly. No reason to go fast here. Even if Durwood was done with Mickey Not-So-Smart, the federal agent wasn't going to come anywhere near the restroom right away. Not because he wanted to give her some space, but because he didn't want to have to deal with her if she broke down.

Which she refused to do. One loss of emotional control per day was well above her usual quota.

She nudged open the door with a knuckle. There wasn't as much blood as she had feared. Four large drops next to the toilet and several smudges around the toilet tissue holder. The roll of paper was gone, and she assumed that it must have had blood on it, too.

She tried to picture Megan cutting herself. Megan who couldn't stand the sight of blood, who had a hard time removing a splinter from her finger.

Jillian's chest tightened as she imagined her sister locked inside the cubicle. Where had the kidnappers been? Outside? Jillian's eyes narrowed. Why would they have allowed Megan to come into the restroom alone? Wouldn't they have been worried that she might escape? With their faces all over the news, why would they have risked coming here at all? Jillian dragged in a deep breath. Because they hadn't been worried about being recognized? Because as Durwood had suggested, the two men whose composites made every news report—those two monsters no longer had her sister and the other women?

How were they ever going to find Megan if they didn't have the right faces or the type of vehicle?

Jillian stepped into the stall, her knees brushing the

toilet bowl as she tried to avoid the blood on the floor. As she turned to close the door behind her, she saw Rick standing five feet away, his hands shoved into the pockets of his jeans, his shoulders hunched just enough that the ends of his hair touched the collar on his coat. Why was it that when she was around him, she felt stronger and weaker at the same time?

Ducking her head, Jillian closed the door. Keeping her eyes down, she inhaled and exhaled several times in preparation. It felt as if she had trapped Megan's fear, her desperation into the small cubicle.

And then Jillian lifted her gaze, her chest tightening all over again, her knees going soft on her. Jillian reached out desperately with both arms, using the sides of the stall to steady herself.

She knew Rick had been surprised when Megan left Jillian's number instead of writing her own name or even the word *help*. Jillian hadn't been. Megan had always turned to her, had always trusted her in a way no one else ever had, even their parents. Even now when Jillian couldn't do a damn thing, Megan reached out to her. Trusting that Jillian would save her.

"Jillian?"

Jillian ripped open the door and stumbled out, straight into Rick's arms. He pulled her in tight, supporting her weight as her legs weakened under her again. God, that was Megan's blood. She'd cut herself, used her own blood to leave Jillian a message. To leave a message to the sister who had left her behind.

"It's okay. I've got you," Rick murmured next to her ear. He kept one arm wrapped around her, anchoring their bodies together, while the other hand slipped beneath her hair to rub her back slowly. "Just take it easy."

But she didn't want easy. Didn't deserve easy. She tried to push out of his embrace, but as he had last night in the hallway, he refused to let her go—not until the sounds of approaching footsteps were heard at the entrance.

As Jillian and Rick each stepped back, McDaniel and Durwood escorted Cory Prescott into the restroom.

Prescott was both younger and better groomed than Mickey and not nearly as nervous. He'd bailed out Mickey Smart because Mickey's wife had asked him to. Evidently, Mickey not only had a drinking problem, he also had three kids under ten years of age and a wife who'd just been laid off from her job.

Prescott had left a few minutes before five because his other job had called, and they needed him in by 6:00 a.m. to open up. "I don't mind helping someone out, keep them from getting fired. As long as it doesn't cost me my job."

Durwood pulled out the composites and the photos again. "Did you see any of these people in here last night?"

The first photo that Durwood passed was of Debra Wert. Prescott stared at it for several seconds, and then with a shake of his head, passed it back. The next was of Megan.

"What about her? Was she in here last night?"

Prescott answered almost immediately. "Yeah."

Even though she didn't realize it, Jillian must have made some sound, because Prescott looked at her. And so did the others. Jillian would have edged forward if Rick's fingers hadn't wrapped loosely around her arm at that moment.

"What time was she here?" Durwood asked, forcing Prescott to focus on him again.

"Probably an hour before I left. Maybe between three forty-five and four." He handed the sketch back. "What's going on here?"

Durwood ignored the question. "Was there anyone with her?"

"Her husband and another man." Prescott looked more nervous now.

"How did you know it was her husband?"

"Because he said so. She was sick. He wanted to go into the restroom with her. I wouldn't let him, so he handed her a paper sack and told her to make it quick. That she needed to change and wash her face and all. Which I thought was odd."

"So he stood outside while she went in?"

"For about five minutes, then he went in after her."

"And you didn't try to stop him?"

Prescott looked worried. "The guy was six-two, with arms as thick as my thighs and a friend for backup. It wasn't as if anyone was in there besides his wife. Or that anyone was likely to show up at that time of morning."

"Did you stick around until she came out?"

"Yeah," Prescott answered, still looking uncertain.

"How did she seem?"

"Maybe slightly scared. Her hand was bleeding. She'd wrapped some toilet paper around it. I asked how she was and she said she was fine. I figured it was some kind of domestic thing."

Durwood handed Prescott the composites. "Were these the two who were with her?"

Prescott nodded. "Yeah."

"Did you see the vehicle they were in?"

"No."

Jillian had been standing there listening to the calm answers, everything inside her twisting into a giant knot. "I don't understand. Why didn't she say something to you? Why didn't she ask for help? Why did they make her change clothes?"

"Not now, Jillian," Rick said, and tried to pull her toward the door. She broke free. "Special Agent Durwood, I want answers. And I want them now."

Rick took her by the upper arms. "Maybe you gentlemen could give us a minute here?"

By the time she was alone with Rick, she was shaking so badly that she could barely stand. "I don't understand. Why didn't she ask for help? If he was right there? If he asked if she was okay? Why wouldn't she—?"

Rick released her. "Men like these two are masters at manipulation. If there had been a cop car out there with an officer standing beside it last night, she wouldn't have said a word."

"But why? She had to know the guy would do something. All she had to do was…"

"What she did. Leaving that message on the back of that door took extreme courage." Rick rubbed his face tiredly. "Especially considering they probably threatened to kill you if she did anything."

"Kill me?"

Rick ran a hand through his hair. "That's how they control their victims. With threats directed at someone the victim loves."

Jillian sagged against the wall. "But why was she

brought here? Why did they make her change clothes?" She lifted her eyes to Rick's. What she saw in them stopped her heart. Pity. Compassion. Regret.

"She's probably not what their original buyer ordered," Rick said quietly, his hands anchored behind her neck now, dragging her back into this arms.

Jillian clenched her eyes closed, waited for the rest of what Rick had to say.

"They may have a buyer for her. To get top dollar, she'd need to be cleaned up."

Chapter Thirteen

Wednesday, 12:03 p.m.

Jillian sat in the SUV. Even though heat poured from the vents, she couldn't stop shaking.

It was still early, but Rick was checking them in to the Happy Camper Lodge, a mom-and-pop motel not far from the rest area, the same one where Durwood and McDaniel were staying.

With the frosting of wind-driven snow, the low-slung log structure looked more like a gingerbread house than a motel. The door to each unit was painted a different vibrant color and beneath each window a flower box held artificial mums and ivy.

Staring out the window that was quickly becoming coated by the snow, Jillian fiddled with the cell phone in her lap. Rick's word's haunted her. *If Megan had been sold to someone already...*

Jillian rested her head back against the seat. More and more she felt as if she was never going to see her sister again. And even if she did, even if they found Megan, how was either one of them going to survive what had happened to her?

Tears leaked down Jillian's cheeks when Rick opened the driver's door. Not wanting him to see them, she swiped at her cheeks. As he pulled the door closed, the scent of his aftershave and the clean, cold air laced with pine filled the interior. He wore his usual white shirt beneath the leather jacket. On most men it would have made him look tame, like a banker or an accountant, but on Rick the conservative choice of shirts made him appear more…dangerous. An image that his unshaven face and the intensity of his dark gaze perpetuated.

He reached for the ignition. "They only had one room left. I took it." He turned the key. "We're more likely to get information as it comes in if we hang close to Durwood and McDaniel."

She nodded. "That's fine."

Though her body desperately needed rest, she doubted that even if she had a room of her own she'd be able to sleep. Since Monday night her life had become one big long panic attack.

Jillian looked out the side window as Rick backed out of the parking spot in front of the motel office.

"Do you think it's possible that if they…if Megan is with someone else now, they might be close by? Somewhere around here?"

"No. Unfortunately, I don't think we can assume that," he answered.

That's one of the things she liked about him. He was honest even when it was hard to be.

Rick pulled the car around to number thirteen. Jillian had never been superstitious, but when Rick held open the red door, she found it difficult to step inside. But she did.

The interior walls were log also, and when combined

with the wide-plank wooden floors the room seemed cozy in spite of the lingering dampness. A brightly colored quilt on the queen-size bed added life and warmth, as would the gas fireplace once it was lit.

Rick dropped his duffel bag onto the end of the bed. "Do you want to go get something to eat, or would you prefer to rest while I get us something?"

They'd both had crackers out of the vending machine. He'd eaten his. She'd managed to eat half of hers by washing it down with a cola. In spite of that, she wasn't hungry. But unless she wanted to stay in the room by herself, she was going to have to pretend to be.

"I could use something. Just let me splash some water on my face and I'll be ready."

When she came back out of the bathroom, Rick was sitting on the end of the bed, the television on. Seeing the composite drawings of the kidnappers flash on the screen, she immediately turned back to the sink vanity.

As she finished drying her face, she watched Rick in the mirror. His dark hair had fallen onto his forehead and his five-o'clock shadow was even darker than normal. What would it feel like beneath her hands, or abrading her cheek? She didn't want to be aware of him physically, but she was. And since the kiss last night, it was even worse.

There was no denying the raw chemistry of physical attraction. Or that when he held her, she felt safe, but she shouldn't be feeling any of those things. Not with Megan missing.

Turning off the television, Rick stood. "After we get some food, we'll get some warmer clothes."

The snow had picked up during the few minutes they'd been inside and was coming down pretty heavily now.

As Rick opened her car door, McDaniel caught them. "A local cop thinks he's found the truck. It's abandoned in the woods about ten miles north of here. If you want, you can follow me."

The fear inside her was just as strong this time as it had been two nights ago. Jillian leaped onto the running board so she could see McDaniel over the roof of the Explorer. "Was anyone in it?"

"Afraid not," McDaniel said as he ducked into the dark sedan. In the next instant the engine turned over and he was backing out.

"Get in," Rick said. By the time they made the entrance, McDaniel's taillights were barely visible. Rick punched the accelerator.

Because of the snow, the winding country roads and one wrong turn, the trip took twenty-two painful minutes with Jillian's heart blocking her throat the whole time. Just as the grave had been empty, the truck was now empty. It felt like a shell game that couldn't be won.

Even as they pulled in behind McDaniel, the federal agent was already out of the car and striding uphill. Because snow coated everything, including the trunks of the trees and the truck, it took Jillian several seconds to spot the vehicle thirty yards above them. If not for the men moving around the truck, she might not have.

Rick glanced at her. "I know it won't do any good to point out that the weather is brutal. That we already know the truck is empty, and that there hasn't been time for Durwood to learn anything."

"You're right. It won't."

She was reaching for the door handle when his hand

on her left forearm stopped her. Something in his eyes
made her sink against the seat back again.

"Punishing yourself isn't helping your sister."

"That's not what I'm doing."

"Sure it is." He turned and looked up the hill. "I saw
your eyes this morning when you stumbled out of that
stall. Forcing yourself to confront Megan's message
didn't help her, it just harmed you."

"Harmed me how?"

"You're not as tough as you think." His mouth tightened. "None of us is," he added as he zipped his coat.

As soon as she stepped out, the wind tore at her clothing
and dragged her hair across her face. Scraping it back, anchoring it behind her ears, she started up the slope.

Rick was wrong about the reason she'd walked into that
stall this morning and the reason she was climbing this hill
right now. It wasn't about punishment. It was about taking
back what the kidnappers had stolen from her. For two
days she had felt powerless. The only way she knew to
fight the sense of helplessness was to confront it head-on.
Seven years in foster care hadn't made her a victim. This
wasn't going to, either. Rick was right about thing, though.
She wasn't nearly as tough as she'd once thought.

But what had he meant by his last words? *None of
us is.* What had made him feel powerless? His father's
murder? Or something else?

The ground was slick and uneven. Almost as soon as
she started scrambling up the steep slope, her thigh
muscles were burning. Obviously there was another
way to reach the truck, a drive, an opening in the trees
of some sort, but thanks to McDaniel that wasn't the
approach they were on.

She could hear Rick climbing behind her, his steps dislodging loose rubble. When her foot skidded on the frozen ground, Rick grabbed her hand and pulled her with him as they climbed the rest of the way.

At the top she doubled over, catching her breath for several seconds. Straightening, she studied the truck. Yellow crime-scene tape fluttered in the wind, but she ignored it, staring at the vehicle. Road dirt made it appear almost gray. The white paint that had been used to conceal the original lettering had started to peel, revealing splotches of black and red.

"Come on." Rick's hand closed under her elbow. "We need to follow this path."

Looking down, she saw where numerous footsteps had ground the snow away. When they reached the back of the truck, instead of being open, the rear door was rolled shut.

Durwood had been talking to McDaniel and some local cops, but when he saw them, he walked over.

Jillian hugged her arms in front of her. "Can I see the inside please?"

From the look that Rick and Durwood exchanged, Jillian knew they planned to turn her down. Somehow she was going to have to change their minds.

"I need to know she's not in there." Jillian tightened her arms in front of her. She had no intention of backing down. Maybe Durwood saw as much, because he turned and shoved the door up, the sound going through her.

As she stepped forward to look, a breeze whipped inside, stirring the straw, buffeting the wire mesh dividers. The partially buried empty manacles glinted in the bedding and the next breeze carried the scent of urine.

She fought to keep her breathing even.

Rick pushed in front of her and jerked the door down. "The evidence needs to be preserved."

Turning away, she wondered if that was the real reason, though. Or if he had sensed her distress. The door had been up for less than thirty seconds, but somehow in that half minute the panic inside her hadn't improved as she'd hoped—it had simply escalated to the next level.

"Jillian?" Rick's voice rumbled from just behind her.

Ducking her head, she faced him. "I'm fine." She wasn't, of course. Maybe he was right. Maybe she was just punishing herself. But she didn't know how to stop.

Durwood rejoined them. "Engine block is cold. They probably made the switch shortly after they left the rest area this morning. The ground's pretty frozen, so there isn't much in the way of footprints to tell us if the women were conscious when they were transferred." Durwood glanced uphill, toward the deeper woods above them. "I have men up there now, checking for any signs of digging."

She followed his gaze. Durwood was looking for a grave, or graves. The idea that Megan had been sold had filled her with terror, but Jillian now realized that as long as Megan was worth something to the kidnappers, she would remain alive. And as long as she was alive, there was hope.

But what about Debra Wert? Why would they want to kill her? Wouldn't they want to sell her, too?

Jillian turned back. "Why kill Debra Wert and not my sister?"

Both men looked at her, then at each other.

"That's a good point," Rick said. "What if she wasn't just at the wrong place at the wrong time like Megan and Jillian? What if she was kidnapped for another reason? Something more personal?"

Durwood's mouth thinned. "Langley's been checking into the sales calls Debra Wert made on Monday, but with this being a holiday week, he's running into some problems. Nearly half the smaller travel agencies have closed early for Thanksgiving. He's caught some of them at home, but many of them are out of town."

"In other words, don't expect any help from that direction until next week?"

Durwood's mouth compressed into an even tighter line. "For now, we'll stay focused on what we do have. Once the truck gets hauled back to the lab, the guys will go over it. Maybe we'll turn up something. Maybe Megan left us something else." He glanced at Jillian, cleared his throat. "I'll make sure you know something as soon as I do. I know how hard this is for you. And I'm sorry that we got off to a rocky start yesterday."

Jillian nodded, surprised by the apology. "Thanks," she said solemnly.

Rick blew on his hands to try to warm them. "Any way to tell if they were in one or two vehicles when they left here?"

Durwood motioned toward the narrow lane the truck had used. "One set of tire tracks. Doesn't completely eliminate the possibility that a second vehicle remained on the pavement, but I doubt it."

"Well, with seven women and the two men, it's got to be some type of panel van or motor home. Something where the women wouldn't be seen." Rick glanced at Durwood. "What do you think? Panel van? Most likely white?"

"The kind favored by every plumber, electrician and phone-repair company?" Durwood said. "Exactly."

Wednesday, 2:22 p.m.

AS SOON AS THEY WALKED into the hotel, Jillian headed to take a shower. On the way back they'd grabbed a sandwich and stopped at a small discount store to pick up heavier coats and gloves. The kidnappers were heading north, which meant Rick, Jillian and the task force would be doing the same. And the weather forecast was calling for heavy snow.

After turning on the gas fireplace, Rick called Langley for an update. He'd just hung up when Jillian came out of the bathroom. She wore another pair of jeans and a black turtleneck sweater that he suspected she'd chosen because it concealed the signs of Gardner's attack.

He noticed that she carried her cell phone. She rarely put it down, nor did she stuff it into a pocket. She didn't say it, but he knew that she was hoping Megan would find some way to call. And maybe Jillian was right. The connection between the two women was extremely strong.

He recalled the wording on the psychologist's report. Difficulty bonding. He hadn't seen any signs of that. At least, not where Jillian and Megan were concerned.

"What did Detective Langley have to say?" Jillian sat on the rug before the fireplace, legs crossed in front of her, the phone cradled in her lap.

"No real news yet. No calls on the composites of the kidnappers."

"What about the lists you and Langley talked about compiling last night? Of the people connected to the

Midnight Run Murders, your dad's death and what's happening now?"

"Six names showed up on more than one list, and there were two people who appeared on three."

"Who showed up on three?" she asked.

"Dan Stebbins, a detective with the sheriff's office and Tim Maley, Charleston County's medical examiner." Rick didn't believe either man was involved, but if he had to put money on one, it would have to be the M.E. Not so much because he believed Tim Maley was involved, but because Rick couldn't see Dan Stebbins getting twisted up in kidnapping, white slavery and murder. He knew Stebbins, had met him on several occasions.

As far as clearing any of the names, Langley was running into the same problem as with checking out Debra Wert's sales calls. People were out of town. Wouldn't be back until Monday.

"I need to talk to you about something," Rick said, trying to navigate the best approach to what he had to say.

She turned toward him, the fire at her back now, her eyes revealing jut how nervous those few words had made her.

"What Durwood is doing, allowing us to be involved, that's not how it's usually handled. I'm sure you know that."

She ran her fingers over the bristles of the hairbrush. "And you're worried if I push too much, that might change?"

"Something like that."

She nodded. "Okay. I'll try to keep that in mind."

She studied him instead of the fire for several seconds. "Why did you give up being a cop?"

The question caught him off guard, but he didn't hesitate to answer. "My wife didn't like the hours." Nor had she wanted to be married to a cop. Which was odd, because when she'd finally left him, he'd been studying to take the bar and the man she'd left him for was a detective with Charleston PD.

He leaned forward, resting his elbows on his knees. "Why did you choose law?"

It wasn't just firelight playing across her face now; she was debating if she would tell him the truth, or if she would give him the answer she gave total strangers.

He waited to hear which it was, and was surprised how much it mattered.

"My adoptive father was an attorney. I wanted to please him, to make him proud, and that seemed the easiest way."

"And was he pleased?"

She nodded. "Yeah. The day I was adopted was probably one of the best days of my life, but the day I graduated was a close second."

He was slowly piecing together her life. She'd had a rough childhood, but instead of letting it define her, she had somehow managed to rise above it. She gave the credit to the Sorensens, but he suspected it had more to do with Jillian.

Though he tried not to, Rick watched as Jillian dragged the brush through her wet hair in measured strokes.

Arching her back, she shrugged the kinks out of her shoulders. Briefly the sweater pulled across her breasts. Rick felt his body tighten. What would it be like to peel the turtleneck off her, exposing more skin to the fire's warmth, to his gaze? He imagined undoing her jeans.

Would she make that sound in her throat again as he eased them from her hips, that hitch and sigh thing that had nearly driven him over the edge last night?

Rick forced himself to look out the window. Those were dangerous thoughts for a man sharing a room with a woman. Especially the first woman in a long time to make him want to discover any of those things.

"Maybe you should try to get some rest," Rick suggested. Anything to get her out from in front of the fireplace. "There's not much we can do for now. I'm going to catch a shower." A long, cold one.

When he came out of the bathroom nearly fifteen minutes later, she was stretched out on one side of the bed, completely dressed and with the extra quilt tucked beneath her chin.

He glanced at the chair in the corner, and then, because he needed sleep, because if a call came, no matter what time it came, they would all be on the move again, he stretched out next to her.

Still asleep, she murmured something indistinguishable and scooted backward until her buttocks rested against him. At first contact, Rick drew in a sharp but shallow breath, not surprised to find that all it took to undo twenty minutes of cold-water torture was Jillian's firm backside anywhere near him.

With nowhere else to put his hand, Rick rested it on her hip and closed his eyes.

When he woke up, firelight played on the beams overhead. And the sound of a television leaked through the wall from McDaniel's room. A car door slammed several rooms away.

Rick checked his watch. No reason to get up yet. No

reason to disturb Jillian. But he couldn't resist turning on his side to face her. She wasn't asleep, as he had expected.

"Hey," she said, her voice low, laced with a sleepy, seductive quality.

"You slept some."

"Mmm." She sat up, pushed the hair away from her face. "What time is it?" She looked down at him. Her eyes were dark, the lids still heavy. And perhaps, because she wasn't quite awake, she seemed relaxed. Almost as if she hadn't yet remembered why they shared a bed.

"Eight o'clock." Because he couldn't stop himself, he reached up, his hand sliding beneath her thick hair to cup the back of her neck. She didn't resist when he urged her mouth down to his.

He swallowed the soft hitch that escaped her lips, and briefly deepened the kiss before pulling back once more. "Tell me to stop." Even as he said those words, he hoped that she wouldn't. Stopping was the last thing he wanted to do.

Her gaze remained locked on his face. And then after several seconds, instead of speaking, she lowered her mouth toward his hesitantly.

It was all the answer he needed. His hand locked behind her neck again, pulling her down, spilling her body over his as he devoured her mouth.

Her leg tangled with his. He needed to feel warm skin. His hand slid beneath the sweater to cup her breast. She immediately arched into the pressure, her lips opening even wider beneath his. Rick released the catch at the front of her bra, giving him what he really wanted, free access to her body. Her nipples were already hard, nearly as hard as he was.

He shoved the sweater out of the way, his mouth replacing his fingers. She groaned as his lips closed over her nipple.

He knew he was moving too fast, but couldn't stop himself. He released the button on her jeans. As his hand moved downward, the zipper gave way. He pushed beneath her panties, the ones he'd watched her buy. The ones he'd been picturing her in for nearly two days.

She exhaled sharply as he found the very core of her, and he allowed himself to believe that she'd been waiting for him. She was breathing fast. But nothing like he was. His pulse thundered in his ears. He wanted to be inside her. Wanted to feel those strong feminine thighs wrapped around him. Wanted to feel her slick wetness…

He reclaimed her mouth. How much longer would he be able to hold out? And how was he going to leave her long enough to retrieve the condom from his wallet on the dresser?

Blood pounded in his head, in every vein in his body. It was as if he were on fire, the need to be inside her consuming him.

"Don't move."

Halfway to the dresser, halfway to salvation, someone pounded at the door. For a brief moment he thought about not answering it, but of course that wasn't an option.

By the time he turned back to the bed, Jillian was already scrambling toward the bathroom.

Rick allowed himself another few seconds to get it together before answering the door.

Frigid air hit him in the face. McDaniel stood there in the dim light. When he looked at Rick speculatively, Rick realized that the federal agent had a clear view of the rumpled bed and probably knew full well what he'd interrupted.

"What is it?" Rick asked.

"Just got a call. A hundred and twenty miles north of here, a couple of hunters found a woman in a shallow grave. The local cops think it may be Debra Wert. You can ride with me if you want."

"We'll follow."

When Rick turned around, Jillian was already lacing up her hiking boots. Done with that, she switched to cramming her things into the new tote bag as if she were stuffing a turkey.

Obviously she had no intention of meeting his gaze or discussing what had just taken place.

But he didn't think for a moment that she'd be able to forget it. He sure as hell wasn't going to be able to anytime soon.

Chapter Fourteen

Even though Rick was at the wheel, Jillian stared intently at the road ahead of them. The wet snow floated into the SUV's headlights, obliterating the glow of the red tail-lights in front of them for several seconds at a time.

The windshield wipers slammed back and forth, a metronome that her heart kept pace with. The driving conditions out on the interstate had been better; at least they hadn't needed to cope with the sharp, sudden curves of the country roads.

Jillian glanced at Rick. Both of them had adamantly avoided any mention of what had taken place, but it had ridden with them in the warm confines of the car. She tried to tell herself that it wasn't important. That she'd been reaching out, desperate to feel anything but the fear. But she knew better. If it had been anyone else in that bed tonight, it wouldn't have happened.

It had been nearly a year since she'd done much dating. Between taking care of her father and studying for the law bar, there hadn't been time. Nor had she met anyone who had tempted her to make the time. Certainly no one like Rick Brady.

As the car took the next curve, Jillian's backside slid to the right, toward the door. For the past few moments she'd been white-knuckling it, and at the same time praying that it was Debra Wert in the shallow grave and not Megan. Jillian didn't try to sort out if that made her a bad person. She'd already accepted that it only made her human. Death affected everyone in pretty much the same way. The closer to home it struck, the more deeply it was felt.

Suddenly the car in front of them took a sharp right, appearing almost to have skidded off the road.

"Hold on," Rick said tensely as he followed the vehicle into the narrow drive. Trees whipped past. The Explorer dove and then immediately seemed to lunge up the sharp gravel incline opposite. Tires spun, gouging for traction, the gravel spray from the car in front pinging against the SUV's front end. It was like chasing a bat into hell.

Brake lights flashed in front of them. Rick swerved to the left, braking hard. As they climbed the next rise, though, the wall of trees suddenly disappeared and they were on top of a hill with a cornfield spread before them. Half a dozen cars had pulled in at odd angles, almost as if they'd just completed a round of bumper cars.

If there was such a place as the middle of nowhere, they had just reached it.

Rick handed her one of the flashlights. "Stay with me at all times."

She didn't bother to tell him that she had no intention of letting him out of his sight. That even surrounded by people, the woods and the remote location reminded her too much of another woods, another night.

They climbed out at the same time, into air so cold that it burned the lungs. She'd pulled on two sweaters and the insulated coat, but it still wasn't enough. Even her feet, encased in heavy socks and boots, felt the cold seeping up from the frozen ground. She should have bought a hat today, too, she realized. Rick had—a black western one that he grabbed from the backseat.

McDaniel's headlights were still on and he stood in the glaring brightness waiting for them. As soon as they reached him, he wordlessly set off at a fast pace, keeping to the furrow between two rows of dried stalks.

The snow came down heavier now, the gusting wind swirling it skyward, almost as if they were encased in a snow globe that was being rocked side to side.

"Have you been listening to the weather reports?" McDaniel asked without slowing down.

From Ohio to Pennsylvania and as far east as New York state, the area was expected to receive more than a foot of snow, accompanied by gusting winds and single digits.

Jillian lengthened her stride. "Do you think they'll actually close the interstate?"

McDaniel glanced back. "If this keeps up, they will."

She could feel Rick watching her, but she continued to concentrate on the ground, on staying on her feet. As much as she didn't want it to be the case, one part of her mind couldn't quite let go of what had happened back at the hotel.

She was brought up short when a rabbit darted across

her path and disappeared into the brush at the edge of the field. Lifting her flashlight, she scanned it toward the trees.

A sense of déjà vu swept over her. On the night of the attack, even before the kidnapper had shown himself, she'd known he was out there watching them. Jillian's hand tightened on the heavy flashlight. And she had that same feeling now.

She looked back around, expecting to see McDaniel and Rick only a few feet in front of her, but when she'd stopped, McDaniel hadn't slowed down, and even Rick, who was deep in conversation with the federal agent, hadn't noticed that she'd dropped back.

Jillian hurried to catch up.

McDaniel suddenly cut across the rows, heading for a slight opening in the trees ahead. Instead of bare frozen soil, their footsteps crunched dried grass and leaves and brush buried beneath the snow.

Ahead, she could see the glare of portable floodlights, this system she assumed, because of its silence, powered by batteries.

Even God couldn't have turned night into day any more effectively.

In the distance, dogs alternately yipped and bayed, reminding her that it was hunting season. That it had been hunters who'd found the grave.

A group of a dozen or more people stood just ahead. The two men wearing camo fatigues were probably the hunters who had found her, the rest local law enforcement.

As they got closer, Durwood saw them and turned, separating himself from the others.

He still wore the camel coat, but the polished shoes had been replaced with a pair of old hiking boots, and a navy-blue ski cap had been added. His long, angular face was beginning to show the same types of signs of fatigue she'd seen in Detective Langley's face last night. She couldn't remember the last time she'd looked really closely in a mirror, though, and figured she probably looked worse than either of them.

Durwood held out his hand to her and then to Rick.

"One of the dogs got to her, dug her up partially before being called off. From what I can see, it's possible that it's Debra Wert. I know it's going to be difficult, Jillian, but I was hoping that you would take a look. Give us a positive ID?"

She nodded. "Okay." Jillian's heart pounded, not from the hike, but because she knew that even though it wasn't Megan, it still wasn't going to be easy to see Debra Wert. Two nights ago their lives had become permanently linked.

"Any idea how long she's been there?" Rick asked.

"Not long. When the first responding officer checked for a pulse, her skin was still warm. In this kind of weather, that probably means no more than an hour. Maybe less."

"But the hunters didn't see anything?"

"Unfortunately, no. And wouldn't have spotted the victim except for the dog. If it hadn't been hunting season, she could have lain out here for months, maybe forever, so finding her at all is a gift."

A gift. Jillian shoved her hands into her pocket. She found the word *gift* and a dead woman's body being used in the same sentence very uncomfortable.

The wind grabbed at Rick's hat, forcing him to hold on to it. "Is it possible that someone traveling the road saw something?"

"Local law enforcement is canvassing a few of the farms near here, to see if anyone noticed an unfamiliar vehicle parked up here around that time. But several of the families have gone off for the holiday."

Jillian stamped her feet, trying to warm them. "It took us two hours to get here. If they left the rest area at five this morning, what have they been doing all day? Why has it taken them so long to get here?"

Even as she said it aloud, she knew. They'd been busy selling Megan. Jillian's hands balled into fists inside her pockets where no one else could see them. Where was her sister right now?

Durwood didn't offer that explanation, though. "They don't appear to be in a great hurry. That or maybe they've just been taking a very erratic route, in hopes of evading detection."

Durwood ducked his head briefly. "In the good news department, that puts us only about three hours behind them right now, and with this storm coming in, most people will be staying off the roads. So either they'll find someplace to dig in, or they'll be out there where we can find them."

Durwood paused to suck on a lozenge. "The jurisdictions north of here have been contacted. Every officer out there tonight will be looking for our suspects." He turned away, heading back in the direction he'd come from. "Let's get this over with so you can get out of this cold."

For the past two hours she'd been steeling herself for this moment, and as much as she dreaded it, she was also eager for it to be behind her. As she followed Durwood, Rick stayed right with her, and McDaniel dropped in behind. The cluster of gathered men parted, allowing them to flow through. In some of the eyes she saw what she'd been feeling for days now. Fear. Uncertainty. A sense that everything was wrong in the world.

A black tarp covered the area. Durwood reached down and rolled it back, almost as if he turned down a bed.

The first thing Jillian saw was the blond hair that was a slightly paler shade than Megan's. Debra's eyes were closed, almost as if she were asleep. Her face and shoulders were partially uncovered, as if the soil had purposely been tucked beneath her chin like a blanket. But her lower body remained hidden from view. Except for her left calf. It was almost as if she'd stuck it out from beneath the covers to cool her body down. Here and there, the pale blue suit peeked through the soil.

As if in a hurry to replace the cover, Durwood held on to the corner of it. "Is it Debra Wert?"

Jillian nodded. Her throat was too tight to speak.

Rick's hand rested at the center of her upper back. "Come on. There's nothing more you can do here."

Less than forty-eight hours ago, Jillian had stood in similar woods, listening to those same words from Rick. What about after the next forty-eight hours had passed? Would he suggest that there was nothing more she could do for her sister? That she should give up? Go home? Wait for a phone call or news?

How did anyone ever let go? Jillian inhaled. They didn't. No matter how much they may appear to have moved on, they hadn't. There would be one dark corner of their mind where they still prayed, where they still believed in miracles. As she did.

Rick's fingers splayed wider on her back then dropped away. "Jillian? It's time to go." He was ready to leave, probably anxious to escape the brutal cold. But then, it was easier for him to walk away.

Her gaze connected with Durwood's. Just as it was easy for the federal agent to stand next to the grave, the expression on his face one of acceptance.

Jillian steeled herself. "Can I have a few moments?"

"Sure," Durwood said. He left Debra uncovered. "Just don't get too close, okay?" As he walked by, he paused to squeeze her shoulder.

She could feel Rick standing there just behind her, offering silent support as she edged forward.

Kneeling on the snowy ground, Jillian thought about the terror she'd seen in Debra's eyes when she'd run out into the road and in front of their car two nights ago. Tears collected in Jillian's eyes as she thought not only about Debra, but about the woman's family, too.

Jillian pulled the glove off her right hand, left it in her lap.

"I'm sorry," she offered, barely able to get the words out. Jillian's hand crept forward. She remembered Durwood's warning not to get too close, but what harm could there be in a single touch? Hadn't a stranger—a cop—already felt for a pulse? She just needed to say goodbye. Just as she'd said goodbye to her father just over a month ago.

As soon as Jillian's fingers reached Debra's cheek, she realized that something was wrong. She jerked back, pressed her bare palm to her own cheeks. How was that possible? How could her own cheek be nearly as cool as Debra's?

As comprehension found that first important toehold inside her, Jillian took a deep breath, the cold slicing her lungs. "Rick...she's...not..." The words wouldn't come.

As if sensing her distress, Rick stepped past Jillian, dropped onto his knees, his fingers pressing at Debra's neck.

"I've got a pulse here," he yelled. "We need an ambulance. Now!"

Chapter Fifteen

Jillian and Rick waited until after the ambulance pulled away before getting back in the SUV and returning to the interstate. Jillian realized she'd been offering silent prayers for Debra Wert. The woman was a survivor. Strong. To still be alive after all she'd been through...

Despite the fact that the kidnappers had seemed to stay on a northerly track, there was nothing to guarantee that they would continue to. But it was either head north, take the gamble, feel as if they were doing something, or return to the Happy Camper Lodge and wait.

Even though it was unlikely that Megan was still with the other women, they were the only tie Jillian had to her sister now. Rescue the women, apprehend the kidnappers—find Megan.

Otherwise...

Jillian stared out the side window. She couldn't think about *otherwise*.

She glanced down at the phone number for the

hospital that she'd written on one corner of the map. It was still too soon to call and check on Debra Wert.

She rubbed her temples. "I just can't get it out of my head. All that time she was alive, and yet nobody noticed anything."

"It happens." Rick's mouth tightened. "Especially if the first officer on the scene is inexperienced. She was partially buried when he got there. He expected her to be dead. So he didn't check as thoroughly as he should have."

"And a woman could have died."

Her anger wasn't nearly as sharp as it would have been two days ago. Would there come a point when her heart would go numb, would stop aching when confronted with the unthinkable?

Rick reached over, covering one of her hands with his. "Don't get your hopes up, Jillian. She was left for dead. And we don't know how long she'd been out there. Durwood based his time estimate on the first officer's report that she was still warm. But obviously she could have been out there for much longer."

So instead of a three-and-a-half-hour lead, the kidnappers could have a much larger one. Jillian closed her eyes, rested her head against the seat back for several seconds, wallowing in her misery. Then, straightening in the seat, she opened her eyes, marshaled her thoughts into more productive channels. Like looking at the map and figuring out a place for them to stop for the night. There were already news reports about interstates being shut down within the hour.

For the past twenty minutes the snow had gone from coming down hard, to coming so fast that it was like driving into a white wall. Sharp crosswinds rocked the SUV. They'd encountered only three cars. One, a maroon sedan, had just passed them going above the speed limit; the other two vehicles had moved more cautiously, more in line with road conditions.

Rick looked over at her. "Any luck finding a better route?"

"Most of the roads are secondary. There are no real towns coming up. At least nothing right on the highway." Even with the roads as bad as they were, she didn't really want them to slow down.

"What about a town that's not on the highway, but a decent size?"

"Grand Junction is off to the east." She squinted, adding up the mileage numbers. "It's about thirty-two miles once we get off. Roads look pretty winding, too. Maybe we should keep going until they make us get off."

"Damn. Hold on."

Surprised, Jillian jerked her eyes up in time to see two headlights coming straight at them. She stared, her heart going from stop to sixty in a split second. Dropping the map, she grabbed the armrest and held on, preparing for whatever evasive action Rick took.

When he held steady to their current course, she glanced worriedly at him. Why wasn't he reacting? Why didn't he attempt to swerve? To miss the other car?

One moment the white pickup truck was aimed at the SUV, the next it was doing a 360 in their rearview mirror. Jillian turned around and watched over the seat back. Almost immediately, the truck pulled back onto the interstate, but this time, it crept away in the slow lane now.

Rick pulled off the Western hat and tossed it into the backseat. "How soon is that exit for Grand Junction?"

"I think it's the next one coming up."

Thirty minutes later, halfway up a mountain and still climbing, Rick pulled into an overlook. A freezing rain had swept through, turning the roads to ice. He eased the SUV as far off the road as possible.

"I think it's time to cut our losses. Come morning we'll head back the way we came, pick up the interstate again. They'll clear it before the secondary roads."

Accepting that Rick's plan was the only one that made any sense, Jillian shoved the map away and flipped open her cell phone. She waited tensely while it searched for service.

No service.

If Megan tried to call, she'd get voice mail. The same would happen if Durwood tried to contact them. And there was no way that Jillian could check on Debra Wert, either. For the next few hours, everything that mattered was on hold.

How was she going to cope?

Rick adjusted his seat, moving it back as far as possible, and then raised the steering wheel to give himself more room.

"We'll get it warm in here," Rick said as he kicked the heat on high. "And then shut down the engine."

She frowned. "Are we low on fuel?"

"No. We're fine. But with it being a holiday, we might run into some problems finding gas, especially out here in a rural area."

She'd forgotten that it was Thanksgiving. She and Megan had reservations at Charleston Place, one of the nicest hotels in Charleston. They'd actually gone shopping for special outfits last week. The carefree day of trying on clothes felt like a lifetime ago. Jillian found herself smiling sadly, recalling how for the first time since their father's death, Megan had seemed lighter that afternoon. The trip to Charleston, Megan's being accepted at the medical college, Jillian's interviewing with a top firm—everything had seemed as if it had been falling in place for them.

Maybe it had been the same for Debra Wert?

Maybe Debra's family would have more reason to give thanks today. Jillian hoped so. She glanced over at Rick. He'd shifted so that his shoulders pressed against the door and he was watching her.

The hot air blasting from the vents, the soft glow of the dash lights, made the space seem even smaller.

Jillian played with the zipper on her jacket. "Did you have plans for today?"

"Yeah. Some of the guys I went to school with are getting together at Charleston Place. It's sort of a tradition."

Surprised, she looked over at him. "What time was your reservation?"

"Four o'clock."

She frowned. "If none of this had happened, I wonder if we would have seen each other there. Maybe sat at the next table."

"If you and Megan had been anywhere in that dining room this afternoon, you would have been noticed, and probably hit on by every guy at my table." Rick offered a half smile.

She knew that he was trying to make her feel better.

The truth was, if it wasn't for this tragedy, and his own tragedy, his father's murder, they probably would never have met.

She looked up at him. "Isn't it amazing how one moment in time can change everything? I missed a turn. It's such a silly little thing. And yet... It's a turn I'll never forget."

"Maybe not completely. But it will be overshadowed by the day we find Megan."

She glanced up, wanting to believe those words. "Earlier today, you said that none of us are as strong as we want to believe. What did you mean?"

He closed his eyes, rested the back of his head against the window. "That some of us have a hard time reaching out even when we need other people."

"Is that what happened when you lost your father?"

"No." Rick rubbed his face. "That's what happened to my father and me when my mother died. We just stopped talking. It went on for a year, until the first anniversary of her death." He shifted. "You lost your mother when you were very young."

"I was five."

"Do you remember anything about her?"

"No." She did, though, at least some things. But she had long ago discovered it was easier and less painful to just lie. It wasn't as if she could recall important details—the color of her mother's eyes, the sound of her voice. As far as Jillian knew, the only photo of her mother in existence was part of a police report.

Jillian felt the sudden need to escape his gaze, the warm intimacy of the front seat. "Maybe we should try to get some sleep."

"Sure. Why don't you climb in back? I'll be fine up here."

Jillian crawled across the center console and into the backseat.

She stretched out on the cold leather, waited for sleep to overtake her, but it didn't.

It wasn't just thoughts of Megan that chased her, but of Rick, too. Of how close they had come to making love. And of how if McDaniel hadn't picked that moment to knock on the door, she wouldn't be feeling quite as alone as she did right now.

Ten minutes later Rick turned off the engine, and the only remaining sounds were the soft ticks of icy snow striking the car's exterior and the soft howl of the wind.

The dark interior cooled down quickly. As her teeth started to chatter together, she tightened the muscles of her jaw. She was damn tired of being cold.

"It's time to share body heat," Rick said, and got into the backseat with her.

When he lifted his arm, she shifted in tight next to him, tucking her shoulder against his rib cage. His arm lowered around her.

As much as she didn't want to be aware of Rick on a physical level, there was no way that she could be alone with him and not have it uppermost in her mind.

They'd known each other for just over forty-eight hours. Was it possible that she was falling in love with him? Or was it just that she needed someone to hold on to, and he was there? And the physical chemistry was right?

After all, what did they really know about each other?

And then she realized, perhaps they knew each other better than couples who had dated for months.

And then Jillian decided it didn't really matter why she wanted to make love with him. She did, and the hell with any consequences.

"Better?" he asked, looking down at her.

For long seconds neither of them moved, their gazes locked. Then Jillian lifted her mouth hesitantly toward his and waited.

He exhaled sharply, as if he'd been holding his breath. His lips met hers, devoured with excruciating slowness. With gentle thoroughness that was so different from the last time.

She fumbled with the buttons of his white shirt. As soon as she reached warm skin, she allowed her fingers to splay wide as she smoothed the shirt toward his shoulders. As her palms brushed across male nipples, he inhaled sharply.

He eased her across him, so that she straddled his muscled thighs, her hands braced on his shoulders. She sank onto his lap. Closing her eyes, she rocked forward. Even through the double layer of clothing, the friction nearly sent her off.

His hands immediately tightened on her hips to keep her from repeating the motion.

He watched her with a tight smile. "I think we may need to expedite things here."

"Expedite?" Her fingers stilled, started to curl, but then he reached up and dragged her mouth close to his. She could feel the tension in his body.

His warm breath brushed her face, as he slowly smiled. "Yeah. Expedite."

Her jeans were the first thing to go. But even without

them, without her panties, she no longer felt cold. Rough denim abraded her thighs and buttocks.

His hands tugged off her heavy coat. They weren't quite as gentle this time, and she found his controlled roughness exciting. He pushed the double layers of sweater up and out of his way. She peeled them off as he undid her bra. Each touch brought a new thrill, a new level of sensation that pushed her closer to the edge.

Jillian got the zipper to his jeans down. As her knuckles brushed him, he grabbed her wrist.

"Let me," he said tightly. And then suddenly there was nothing but warm skin. She desperately wanted to feel him inside her, would have expected him to want the same thing considering his recent haste. But instead, he pulled her mouth to his, kissed her thoroughly while his cool fingers explored.

She watched as he tore open the condom and rolled it on. She had no idea where it had come from and didn't really care.

Rising on her knees, she shifted forward and slowly sank onto him.

As he filled her, she threw her head back, closing her eyes. She rocked on him slowly.

"Look at me," Rick ordered, his voice tight.

Lowering her chin, she did just that.

"Don't hide from me."

He drove up into her, and within three thrusts, she felt reality slide away, felt the edges of her first orgasm just beyond her reach. She heard a groan, felt certain that it must have been hers, but then Rick suddenly went still beneath her and, grabbing her hips, stopped even her movements. "Let's take a slight breather."

She could feel him hard and throbbing inside her, feel her own feminine muscles contracting around him. What was he trying to do? Drive her completely insane?

The sound of their ragged breathing filled the interior of the car. It was only when he pushed the hair away from her face that she realized her skin was damp. He slid his fingers along her cheeks. "I've never done this. Made love in a car. How about you?"

She shook her head. She didn't want to talk about having sex with other people—she wanted to have it with this man. Over and over again.

"You know what that means, don't you, Jillian?"

Shaking her head again, she ran her hands along his shoulders.

He caught her chin. "That makes us each other's first."

The words went through her. For a few seconds their gazes met, but neither of them spoke.

And then he grabbed her hips again, holding her still as he thrust into her once more. This time he didn't stop.

It was more than an hour later when she collapsed against his chest, her lungs fighting for air. Rick's arms wrapped around her, anchoring her body to his.

She had never felt quite so possessed by a man.

No man had ever taken her as completely as he just had.

Chapter Sixteen

Thanksgiving, 8:45 a.m.

Rick looked up from where he was filling the SUV's gas tank. Jillian had just stepped out the convenience store's front door. As she stood there, looking up at the heavy gray sky, she stretched, flexing backward from the hips. The thick insulated coat concealed her figure, but Rick couldn't stop himself from thinking about her body, about last night.

She walked toward him in a loose stride that ate up ground like a runway model. And she had the looks for it, too. With that strong jawline, that slight, feminine cleft in her chin, and golden-green eyes that were like a bottom-less spring and uncomfortably direct at times, she was by far one of the most beautiful women he'd ever met.

At the moment she was gathering up all that dark hair of hers into a ponytail. He recalled the way his fingers had curled into it as he used it to drag her mouth to his. How it had felt swinging against his chest as she rode him.

Stopping four or five feet from him, she checked him out. "You look as if you're ready to go for a ride, cowboy."

Letting go of the pump, Rick straightened. "What?" Was she suggesting what he thought she was?

Smiling, she motioned at his head. "Your hat. It looks as if you're ready to bust broncs for a living."

Rick reached up and removed the cowboy hat he'd bought yesterday. Taking the hat from him, she settled it on her own head. "I guess maybe I should wear it, since I did most of the riding last night."

Before he could say anything, Jillian turned and climbed back into the car. Which was probably just as well, since he preferred that she not see how her words had affected him.

When he slid behind the wheel a few minutes later, Jillian was closing her cell phone. The hat was gone and so was the smile. In its place was a very somber expression. Had Durwood called back? Had there been some overnight development?

"What's going on?" he asked.

She glanced up, still frowning. "Debra Wert came through surgery okay, but hasn't regained consciousness yet."

"That's still a good sign."

"I suppose."

He wondered what she was thinking. Maybe what was bothering her had nothing to do with Debra Wert. Perhaps she was thinking about her sister. Or even about what had happened between them last night.

He'd thought of little else. Since the moment he'd met her, she had been surprising him at every turn. With her tenacity. With her guts. He didn't think he'd ever met a woman more courageous. But last night had been the biggest surprise of all.

Rick pulled out onto the nearly deserted highway as more snow began to fall. He was beginning to hate snow almost as much as he hated the idea that Jillian wouldn't get the happy ending.

They'd decided to continue north on the interstate until they reached Fairmont, West Virginia, where they planned to get a hotel room and wait for news from Durwood.

They traveled in silence for a while, but the lack of conversation wasn't as comfortable as it had been yesterday. There were too many things being left unsaid between them. But maybe that's the way Jillian wanted it for now. And maybe he understood. Until Megan was found, Jillian's focus needed to remain on locating her sister.

And what about his own focus? Somehow, it had expanded from strictly finding his father's killer to include getting Megan back and to protecting innocent lives. And Rick wasn't sure which one he wanted more. He knew what his father's answer would be. There's nothing more critical than saving a life. Even justice wasn't as important.

Once a cop…

Jillian suddenly sat forward, her eyes focused on the road ahead.

"What is it?"

Jillian pointed. "The sign. Do you see it? *N-E-W C-A-R,* and the rest is covered in snow?"

Many of the road signs they'd passed had been difficult to read, but seeing this one made everything sort of click inside his head.

Slowing, Rick pulled off the highway. "What if

Megan wasn't trying to tell us that her kidnappers had changed vehicles? What if she'd somehow overheard their destination?"

Excitement filled Jillian's face. "The guy on duty said one of the kidnappers went in to get Megan. What if he interrupted her before she'd finished?"

Rick pulled back onto the interstate. "Look for the closest town that begins with *New Car.*"

Thursday, 9:13 a.m.

MEGAN SAT BETWEEN her two kidnappers, her shoulders brushing theirs every time the van took one of the hairpin turns. They were in the mountains now, the van struggling with the steeper sections of the narrow, two-lane road.

Snow blanketed the trees and the sky was a sharp crystalline blue. But she didn't notice the scenery, her eyes focused on the heart-shaped gold necklace swinging from the rearview mirror. Jillian's necklace. The one their mother had given her. The one with the bloodred ruby at its center.

Megan concentrated on the side-to-side movement. When had they taken it from Jillian? When they'd first been captured? Her breathing turned shallow. Or had it been later? When Jillian tried to escape?

Was that the reason they hadn't seemed in any hurry that night? Because they'd killed her sister?

After days of constant fear, she'd thought herself immune, but she wasn't. No matter how bad it seemed, there was always another suffocating layer of terror that could be added.

Squeezing her hands in her lap, Megan faced the worst of all possibilities—that her sister was dead.

Jillian might already be dead, but all Megan could think about was the message she'd left in restroom and that it was very possible that no one was coming for her. That no one had even noticed they were missing. In another week, friends and neighbors in Ohio would start to comment that they hadn't seen the two girls, but even if someone went to the police...

And they'd killed another woman, too.

They'd pulled her out of the back of the van, carried her into the woods and buried her.

And they had made Megan witness it. A lesson on what would happen if she wasn't obedient.

The man behind the wheel, the shorter of her two kidnappers, ran his hand up under her cotton dress. She made no move to stop him. She was beyond caring what they did to her. She was numb and tired and almost wished that they had left her back there in the grave with the other woman.

They pulled into an overlook. Any other time of year, it would have been crowded with tourists, but not today. Today there was only a small motor home parked against the rock wall.

Behind it, towering pines climbed the steep slope. She imagined herself breaking free, dodging those trees as she scrambled up the mountain, losing herself in the silence and peace there. Three days ago she would have been afraid to be alone like that. She would have been frightened by the idea of encountering a mountain lion or bear or some other wild animal. But now she understood—the most frightening animals of all sat beside her. And held her life in their hands.

The tall kidnapper, the one with red hair, got out first, left Megan and the other man in the van. When he was halfway to the other vehicle, the driver of the motor home climbed down, but then waited. She couldn't tell much about him. He was average height and was wearing a camouflage coat and hat.

They had a brief conversation, her kidnapper pointing at the van, the other man flashing a fat envelope. Then the kidnapper walked back toward the van. He opened the passenger door and spoke to his partner. "You stay here. He wants to take a look at her before he'll commit."

Megan was dragged out into the bitter cold. The wind cut through the cotton dress, and she was shivering before the door closed behind her.

He jerked her forward. "You smile, hear? And no matter what he does, you keep smiling."

The man from the motor home walked to meet them. She tried to smile as he looked her over, but she couldn't. It was as if those muscles had atrophied.

When the short kidnapper suddenly joined them, the tall one looked irritated. "I thought I told you to wait with the van."

"I needed to stretch my legs."

Ignoring the other two men, the buyer walked around her slowly, running his hand across her buttocks. He was several inches taller than she was and probably weighed 170 pounds, most of it looking like solid muscle. She tried to block out the reason they were all standing in the middle of a parking lot, but couldn't. She was being sold. Even if this guy looked normal on the outside, somewhere inside his head lurked a monster.

"Did you want to check my teeth while you're at it?" Even as she said it, she didn't know where the courage had come from. Or maybe she did. If Jillian wasn't alive, if Megan was truly on her own, it was up to her now. Either she could go meekly, or she could learn to fight like Jillian.

After all, killing no longer was the worst thing they could do to her.

His gaze met hers briefly before he stepped back.

She could see it in his eyes. He was disappointed in her. Relief washed through her. If she didn't get separated from the others, the women still locked in the back of the van, she wouldn't be alone.

The buyer folded his arms. "I don't know what kind of scam you're trying to run on me, but this isn't the girl in the picture." The buyer backed away.

"She's got the same coloring," the tall kidnapper offered. "And she's fresh. Unused. The other girl…"

"Is younger. And broken in."

The kidnappers exchanged a look. "She's in another van. It's due in tomorrow afternoon."

Backing away, the buyer headed for his motor home. "I'll still buy the other girl. Call me if you want to deal."

The next thing Megan knew she was being dragged back toward the van. The tall kidnapper pointed toward the mountain at their back. "Get the shovel. We'll take her up into those trees. Get rid of her up there."

Stunned, Megan's legs collapsed under her. But as soon as he released her, she was back on her feet, racing to the motor home.

She grabbed the guy from behind. As he spun, she dropped to her knees, her fingers twisted in his camouflage coat. "Please. Please." She was crying now. "They're going to kill me. You have to take me with you. I'll do anything. Anything at all. Whatever you want."

The tall kidnapper jerked her backward. She slammed onto the ground. The short kidnapper immediately locked his hand around her left arm and towed her toward the van.

She kept her eyes locked on the man from the motor home, still pleading.

Chapter Seventeen

Thanksgiving, 5:13 p.m.

New Carlyle, Pennsylvania, wasn't a particularly pretty town and was tucked into the Alleghany Mountains northeast of Pittsburgh.

Rick and Jillian hurried through the front door of the small and historic Pinecone Lodge. The first thing that hit them was the warm stuffiness and the smells coming from the dining room. Because it was Thanksgiving, the hotel's restaurant was crowded, filled with the drone of conversation and the clack of cutlery and dishes. Outbursts of laughter.

A hostess, dressed in a Pocahontas outfit, stood next to the dining room's double doors, a large display of dried cornstalks and pumpkins as a backdrop. Seeing Rick and Jillian, she smiled, obviously assuming that they were there to eat.

"This way," Rick said, heading for a hallway across from where they had entered. Jillian hustled to keep up.

Rick jerked open the conference room door, held it for Jillian.

Where the dining room was noisy and boisterous, this space was somber. The lack of windows and the dark plaid carpeting made the room seem smaller than it actually was. The stuffed and mounted head of a large buck hung on the wall, surrounded by forty or fifty smaller sets of antlers. And there was an underlying scent of mildew. All of which probably contributed to why the meeting room had been available on short notice.

Durwood, Langley, McDaniel and another man, one Rick didn't know, looked up as they entered.

Because of the lousy weather and the difficulty getting flights out of anywhere on the Eastern seaboard, Rick was surprised to see Langley. But Rick suspected that even if it had meant hiring a private jet, the detective would have made it.

It was Langley who separated himself from the group and came to meet Rick and Jillian.

"Special Agents McDaniel and Durwood are getting the computers hooked up. Local law enforcement should be here in a few minutes. They're eating turkey and stuffing with their families at the moment." Langley looked tired like the rest of them. It was obvious that even though he hadn't been chasing developments through five states, he'd been working long hours on his end, too.

"Got a call two hours ago. Looks like Tim Maley, our medical examiner, was the inside contact."

Rick frowned "Was?"

"Yeah." Langley rubbed his face. "Like all the others, someone made sure he couldn't talk. He was found dead this morning. Wife went out for a walk, came back to find him on the kitchen floor. Gunshot wound to the head."

"But she didn't see anything?"

Langley shook his head. "No. After he was hauled out of there, a couple of detectives went out to interview the grieving widow. She cooperated until she figured out that we weren't just looking into her husband's murder, that we were also investigating his possible involvement with kidnapping and murder. She shut up and called a lawyer."

If there had been a wall next to him, Rick probably would have buried his fist in it.

Jillian had remained silent up until now. "Does she understand what might be at stake? That we're talking my sister's life, the lives of other women?"

"Yes," Langley said, his disgust obvious. "She more than understands. But she feels that she has to protect her husband's reputation."

Rick recognized the look on Jillian's face. She would have given anything to have the medical examiner's wife in front of her at that moment to scream at, maybe even to slap. And she wouldn't have been the only one in that line.

"Can't you do something? Anything?" Jillian asked. "To make her talk?"

"We are. It just takes time. And the fact that it's a holiday doesn't help."

Rick rested his hand in the middle of Jillian's back. He would have liked to offer her more in the way of comfort, but knew she wouldn't appreciate it at the moment. Like him, she was too keyed up.

"Did they get anything out of the wife before she stopped talking?"

"Yeah. The names of the men who sit in on the

weekly poker game, a list of the golfing buddies and the ones he goes on hunting trips with." Langley exhaled sharply. "We're talking several dozen names that will need to be checked out. And probably won't add up to anything useful. We're looking at his charge card usage and the airlines. Maybe we'll turn up a connection to this area."

The conference room door opened. A blond man dressed in slacks and a sweater walked in. From the expression on Langley's face, it was obvious that he knew him.

"Here's our local sheriff. Meet Ben Tanner," Langley said.

Before the door could close, a girl who was five or six and dressed like an Native American princess caught it and followed him in, her blond hair bouncing in pigtails. "Daddy."

Sheriff Tanner scooped her up and carried her back outside. When he returned, he looked even more irritated than he had originally. As if upset because his Thanksgiving had gotten screwed up.

It was bad enough when citizens didn't want to get involved. It really rankled when cops acted the same way. Being a cop wasn't a job—it was a lifestyle choice, a commitment.

Rick looked over at Jillian. Something was wrong. He could see it in her eyes. But before he had a chance to ask, she was heading for the exit.

Langley glanced at Rick with a concerned expression. "Is she all right?"

"Sure. She mentioned getting something out of the car."

She wasn't okay, of course. But she wouldn't want other people to know that. And for that reason alone, as much as he wanted to go after her immediately, he didn't. Instead he allowed himself to be introduced to the local sheriff.

Langley motioned toward Rick. "Rick here was with Charleston PD."

"Who are you with now?" Sheriff Tanner asked.

"No one. I'm just an interested party."

Tanner's right brow climbed in skepticism.

Durwood showed up then, offering Rick his hand before turning to Sheriff Tanner. "As you'll quickly discover, Rick Brady is probably one of the best ex-local cops you'll ever work with."

When Rick was finally able to break away, he went looking for Jillian. He found her just outside the back door, her forehead resting against the wood siding, her shoulders heaving.

"Jillian," he said quietly, and reached for her. As soon as he touched her, she turned to him without hesitation. But was it because her emotional pain was too great to bear alone? So great that she would have turned to a stranger? Or did it indicate just how far they'd come over the past two days?

He didn't know what had sent her over the edge, but his heart ached for her. He'd been looking for a reason to hold her all day, but he hadn't wanted it to be like this. Because she was falling apart.

Pulling her in tighter, as if somehow he could absorb her grief, he realized that the last time he'd felt this powerless had been as he watched his father's coffin lowered.

"That little girl. She looked…she looked like Megan."

As he stood there holding her, he desperately searched for words that might comfort her. But sometimes…sometimes there just weren't any. He'd learned recently that the best thing to do for someone you cared about was just to hold them.

Rick looked up as Langley stuck his head out the door.

Langley paused, as if debating if he should interrupt. "You may want to come in here."

Rick nodded but didn't say anything, and after several seconds Langley retreated.

As soon as the door thumped closed, Jillian pushed out of Rick's arms. She scrubbed at her cheeks with her hands and then a sweater sleeve. He didn't know what it was—maybe the look of vulnerability in her eyes, or the way her lips seemed softer——but she was the only woman he'd ever seen who looked beautiful after crying.

He realized that he knew her well enough now to predict what she'd do next.

She inhaled deeply, let it out slowly. "I'm sorry."

"You have nothing to be sorry about." Looping his hand behind her neck, he pulled her in tight to him again. "Breaking down isn't always a sign of weakness. Sometimes it's a sign of how much you love someone." He used a finger to lift her chin. "No matter how much it may feel otherwise, you're not alone, Jillian."

By the time they returned to the conference room, all but McDaniel and the other man, Carmichael, were clustered around a laptop at one end of a conference table. Six feet away, Special Agent McDaniel sat at a second computer, his fingers moving rapidly across the keyboard. Carmichael had set up near the back wall and was currently talking on a cell phone.

As soon as Rick and Jillian entered, Langley broke away and walked toward them, all signs of exhaustion gone. Rick knew what the change meant. Something had happened in the few minutes that he and Jillian had been outside. There had been another break in the case. Possibly a significant one.

"Tanner has identified one of our composites as a guy who works security at a property about ten miles north of here. Officially it's listed as some kind of retreat for Hardell Corporation." Langley nodded toward McDaniel. "He's getting us an aerial view of the property now."

"What do we know about Hardell Corporation?"

"Nothing yet. Durwood has Carmichael working on it." Langley folded his arms in front of him. "At this point what we know is that they're very security conscious, keep to themselves and there's a lot of traffic in and out of there. None of it local."

Rick glanced at Jillian, concerned about how she was doing.

"As we both know," Langley said, "this type of operation requires both security and traffic in order to be successful." Moving to rejoin Durwood and Tanner, Langley motioned Rick and Jillian forward with him. "We're tied into South Carolina's DMV and are going down the list of names that Tim Maley's widow gave us, checking to see if Tanner recognizes any of them."

Tanner and Durwood glanced around as Langley,

Rick and Jillian stepped in behind them, but then immediately went back to what they'd been doing.

"What about him?" Durwood motioned to a face on the screen. "Have you seen him around here?"

Tanner studied the face for several seconds and then shook his head. Another driver's-license photo flashed on the screen, and Tanner quickly nodded. "He was a guest over at the jail a couple of weeks ago. Your guy there," Tanner said and tapped a finger on the composite, "came and picked him up the next morning. Wasn't too happy about it. Said something about privileges being revoked. Of course, at the time I assumed he was talking about the key to the corporate men's restroom or something."

"You're sure it's him, though?"

"After the tourists clear out in October, things tend to be quiet. But even if that wasn't the case, I'd remember this guy. He got into a scuffle with one of my deputies during a traffic stop. That and the South Carolina driver's license made him stand out."

"Over here," McDaniel called over his shoulder. "I've got the aerial view up."

Everyone shifted their attention to the other laptop. The picture was grainy, so much so that it was difficult to see the large, sprawling structure surrounded by dense trees at the center of the screen. But once he'd determined what he was looking at, Rick was better able to pick up additional features. Such as the two wings that jutted off the back of the building, the satellite dish in the trees on the right. The three cars parked in front of the house, two of them light-colored limousines.

"There's only one access road," Sheriff Tanner offered. "Going in on foot is a possibility, but given the weather conditions we have right now, it would be damn treacherous. You'd have to come in from the west. It's probably a three-mile hike."

"So you're saying the best option is a frontal assault." Durwood motioned at the lower part of the screen, where a road was barely discernable.

"Unfortunately so. And just before daylight."

"What do you know about the security?" Rick asked.

"From what I've seen, it's high-dollar stuff."

Langley nodded, his arms folded in front of him, his hands tucked into his armpits. "So you've been inside, then?"

"No. Never had a reason to. But occasionally, when some hiker gets too close, we've been called out."

"You mean someone in the house phones? Wants the hiker picked up for trespassing?"

"Yeah, but not often." Tanner rubbed his jaw, exhaling sharply.

"What happens when you show up?" Rick asked. "Do they allow you onto the property, or do they meet you at the road?"

"Sometimes we've gotten as far as the second perimeter."

Langley frowned. "Second perimeter?"

"Yeah. What you can't see in these photos is the eight-foot-high, electrified security fence." Tanner made a circular motion around the house with his finger.

"And you didn't think there was anything odd about the amount of security they had?" Langley asked.

"Sure I did. But I figured with all the sophisticated

hardware, and the limousine service that ran in there once or twice a week, that there was some kind of government connection." He propped his hands at his waist. "And I could wonder until the cows come home. From a law-enforcement perspective, up until now they've been model citizens. They never gave me a reason to go onto the property."

"Limousine service?" Durwood asked. "From where?"

"The Pittsburgh Airport."

Durwood turned to McDaniel. "Have it checked out. Get the names of anyone who's made that limo trip." Durwood next turned to the other agent. "Carmichael, what's the status on that rundown on Hardell Corporation? I want to know who the principals are within the next hour."

Still on the phone, Carmichael nodded.

Tanner ducked his head. "I guess the only way we're going to know for certain if it's a brothel is to go in. What do you gentlemen need from me at this point?"

"What about floor plans for the house?" Rick asked Tanner. "Any way we could get a set from the building department?"

Rick rested his hand in the middle of Jillian's back, aware of how the current conversation must be affecting her. It was the first time she would have heard the word *brothel.* Up until now, all of them had steered clear of the term. But Rick didn't doubt for a moment that Jillian knew the score, knew that unless rescued, all the women were destined to become sex slaves. It was the reason that even from the beginning she'd avoided asking certain questions.

The current conversation also probably made her

think that in a matter of hours they could have the kidnappers in custody, would be able to beat Megan's whereabouts out of them. Unfortunately, that's not how law enforcement worked.

Even when they had the kidnappers in custody, it could take hours or even days to get a lead on where Megan was being held. And that would be if the kidnappers actually knew anything. There was a strong possibility that when the deal went down very little worthwhile information had been exchanged between the kidnappers and the buyer. Everyone in that type of transaction tended to be very cautious.

"I can try to get you a set of floor plans," Tanner said. "Anything else?"

Durwood frowned. "How many men do you have?"

"Full-time? Nine. None of them with SWAT training."

Durwood glanced over at McDaniel. "See if you can get us a few more men here by morning."

Jillian stepped forward. "You're not planning to wait until then."

"I don't want to wait," Durwood said, "but if we don't have enough men to control the situation, we end up with a bloodbath. And I don't mean just the kidnappers, but the women, too, Jillian."

He glanced at the rest of them. "I don't want any discussion about this operation outside this room. We'll meet outside in the parking lot at 5:00 a.m. I don't expect there to be any discussion at that time, either. We'll pick a spot en route for a last-minute briefing. Understand?"

Durwood looked at Jillian. "It might be best if you stayed behind tomorrow morning."

Time unknown

AFTER HAULING MEGAN UP into the motor home, the man pushed her onto the bed in the back. "Move from here, I'll kill you. Understand?"

Panic filled her chest and kept her thoughts scattered like leaves in a hurricane. She assumed after the way he'd touched her moments ago that he wouldn't waste any time. That he'd rape her immediately.

But at least she'd be alive. She owed him that. He had saved her.

He continued to stand over her, but she was afraid to look up, to meet his gaze.

And then without saying anything else he left her sitting on the bed. She immediately checked out the motor home's small bedroom. Some of the doors on the cabinet above the bed were missing and black garbage bags covered the windows. Megan tugged the short dress down.

The man returned with a roll of duct tape. "My name is Sam. What's yours?"

She debated lying, but didn't. What was the point? As soon as she told him, he forced her onto her stomach, and then wrapped the tape around her wrists five or six times. "I wasn't exactly prepared." Ripping off the end, he smoothed it in place over the other layers of tape, then proceeded to bind her ankles. "I won't gag you for now."

When he was finished, he left her there and climbed into the driver's seat. A few moments later they were on the road.

Megan closed her eyes. As long as he was behind the wheel, he couldn't hurt her. She needed sleep. She needed food. The first was within her power; the second wasn't.

She drifted in and out for what seemed like hours, sometimes comforted by dreams where she and Jilly and their parents were together, and at other times terrorized by the black void of fear that lurked ever stronger in her.

And then she woke in complete darkness and realized they were no longer moving. And that even though she couldn't feel him, he was standing over her.

Thanksgiving, 5:45 p.m.

JILLIAN DROPPED her tote onto the bed. After they'd left the conference room, Rick had stopped by the desk to register them. She'd been surprised when he'd handed her the key. After last night, she'd expected him to get just one room.

Did he regret what had happened between them? Was that the reason they weren't sharing a room?

Her thoughts were all jumbled up inside her. How could she even be worrying about the room situation? What did it matter if Rick got two rooms instead of one?

What kind of woman thinks about hot sex when her sister has been kidnapped?

The kind who's damned scared.

The kind who would use almost anything to block out thoughts about what tomorrow will bring.

The kind of woman who believed she was in love with Rick Brady and damn well didn't know what to do about it.

She understood why Durwood was waiting until morning, she just didn't know how she would keep it together until then.

There was a knock at the door. When she opened it, Rick stood there. "Why don't we get cleaned up and get something to eat. They'll be serving in the dining room downstairs for another hour."

"Sure. I'll meet you there in fifteen minutes."

She showered, blew dry her hair and put on makeup in just under twenty minutes. Granted, she didn't have anything but black jeans and a white sweater to wear, but she could at least do as well as she could with what she had.

Rick had already gotten a table in the corner.

The room was mostly cleared out now, only four small groups remaining, all of them clustered near the expansive window overlooking the mountains and well away from the table where Rick sat.

The decor was more of that same cabiny look, the carpet a deep maroon and the ceiling covered in wide planks of wood and heavy beams. From what she'd gathered, because of the hard terrain, the subzero temperatures and the massive amounts of snow, the area was more crowded in the summertime than at this time of year.

As she got closer to the table, Rick stood. He was also dressed in jeans and another white dress shirt, his hair still damp.

"It's not quite Charleston Place." Rick pulled out her chair. "But it does come with such amenities as chairs, china and cutlery."

Since the meal she'd cooked for them two nights ago, they'd eaten either vending-machine fare or fast food, all of it chased with large amounts of coffee.

His hand briefly touched her shoulder before he took his own seat. "I hope you don't mind, but I went ahead and ordered for us. They were getting ready to stop serving."

The waitress brought wine that Rick obviously had ordered.

Jillian waited until they were alone again before speaking. "I know that Megan probably won't be there tomorrow, even if the other girls are." Without picking it up, Jillian slowly turned the wineglass by the stem. "But we'll be able to find her, won't we? There are ways, aren't there?"

"There are always ways," he agreed, his expression troubled. He reached across the table, grabbed her fingers. "We'll get her."

"And you might as well know now that I have no intention of staying behind." She waited for him to repeat Durwood's words, to tell her that she couldn't go.

"I thought we established that a long time ago," he said quietly. "That you are always as close to the front lines as you can get." He leaned forward. "I do have one favor to ask of you, though."

"What's that?"

"That tomorrow you make an exception and wait in the car until it's all over."

She nodded. She wouldn't, of course. She suspected that he knew as much. She didn't think anyone could ever know her as well he did now. And maybe the same was true in reverse. Maybe she knew him better than most people did.

"Have you ever thought about going back into law enforcement?"

He reached for his own wineglass. "No. Why?"

"Because you're good at it. And because I think you miss it."

He didn't respond to the observation, instead changing the subject. "I checked on Debra Wert. She's doing better, but still isn't conscious."

Jillian had also called the hospital and gotten the same message. She'd even spoken to Debra's mother. Joyce Wert had thanked Jillian for stopping that night in the Francis Marion Forest and had offered her prayers for Megan's safe return.

After dinner, Rick walked Jillian back to her room. When she pulled her key card out, he took it from her and slid it into the electronic lock. She didn't want to be alone, but...

He'd been supportive, kind and a perfect gentleman all day. Maybe if he hadn't been, she could have asked him in.

Holding the door open for her, he handed the key card back. "Well, good night."

His hand settled on the back of her neck, his touch cool on her warm skin. Even though she was determined not to, she couldn't look at him without thinking about what had happened last night in the backseat, a warm flush of heat spreading through her at the memory of his hard thighs beneath her buttocks.

She lifted her chin as he leaned in toward her, and waited to feel his lips on hers.

At the sudden click of the door across from hers coming open, Rick straightened, his hand dropping away. Rick stepped back, nodded at Durwood, who stood in the doorway opposite.

Jillian watched Rick walk down the hallway to his own room, and then she glanced at the federal agent. "Good night."

Closing her door behind her, she leaned against it. It

was just after seven. Ten dark hours stretched ahead of her, filled with so many fears and worries that she wondered how she would survive them alone.

Ten minutes later Jillian climbed into bed. She still hadn't purchased any kind of sleepwear, was still using the white oxford-cloth shirt Rick had lent her the night they'd stayed at the condo.

At eleven o'clock she woke up, though, and couldn't go back to sleep. Getting out of bed, she walked down the hall to his room and knocked softly.

It took him several seconds to answer, presumably because he'd had to pull on jeans. As soon as he saw her, he stepped back and she slipped inside. His room was obviously a clone of hers, but somehow felt entirely different just because he stood in the middle of it, watching her.

His chest was bare and his hair looked as if he'd run his hand through it.

There was a set of house plans spread on the small dinette table near the window, a light pooling down onto them. She realized that he hadn't been asleep, that he'd been studying them.

"I don't want to be alone tonight," she said simply.

Chapter Eighteen

Friday, 4:45 a.m.

Four forty-five a.m. came earlier than usual.

At least it seemed that way to Rick as he carried his coffee toward the SUV. Jillian walked shoulder to shoulder with him and was wearing a black turtleneck, black jeans and a down-insulated coat and hiking boots. She'd pulled her hair back again. Maybe it was practical, but he preferred it down.

He saw her tense at Durwood's approach, but the special agent simply nodded. "Good morning, Jillian. Rick."

Durwood looked jazzed, Rick decided, as if he was in his element. Which was pretty much how Rick felt at the moment. He would be excluded from the initial assault—after all, he was a civilian. His life couldn't be placed at risk. But that didn't keep him from wanting to be in the thick of things, from remembering what it was like.

"Load up," Durwood ordered a few moments later. Car doors opened and closed; engines were gunned to life.

The caravan drove east out of town, the five cars

speeding along the rural roads, past darkened homes where neighbors slept, unaware that their community was about to be forever changed. By tonight, national news would have put New Carlyle, Pennsylvania, on the map—the same way Charleston had been put there eight years ago.

The interior of the car was beginning to warm. Rick glanced over at Jillian. As she cautiously sipped her coffee, she seemed to track the string of taillights ahead of them, cutting through the dark like tracer rounds.

Snowfall had tapered to flurries now, but there was still two inches of new snow on the road to deal with.

Because of airport closures, out of the six federal agents who were expected, three had made it. Would it be enough?

The caravan stopped four miles out of town at a roadside park to rendezvous with Sheriff Tanner and his men. As soon as the task force members had parked, men spilled out of the cars. Trunks were popped open. There was very little conversation, though, each man focusing on what the next few hours would bring. In the back of each of their minds was the knowledge that they might not come home tonight. The soft trunk lighting revealed their faces as they reached in, grabbing artillery like a woman choosing accessories at the department-store counter.

As Rick and Jillian walked toward Durwood's car, where the briefing would take place, McDaniel stopped them. "Even if you're sitting this one out, it might be a good idea to be safe."

He handed Rick two protective vests, one obviously meant for Jillian.

"We got a name back on Hardell Corporation. It's owned by Gilman Martin." McDaniel straightened. "Want to know what his other line of work is? Besides running a brothel?" He reached in and grabbed a Glock, slid it into his shoulder holster. "He has a travel agency. And get this, it's called Ultimate Getaways."

He straightened. "We checked the limousine service. Twenty-five to thirty men a week have been flying into Pittsburgh and taking the limousine service up here. They spend anywhere from two to three days and then they're gone. Lot of repeat business, especially your medical examiner. His name came up on the list almost monthly."

"Any news on Debra Wert's condition?" Jillian asked.

"She's listed as stable but still unconscious."

"So I assume Martin was one of Debra Wert's accounts," Rick said.

McDaniel nodded. "I suppose we'll learn why he wanted her dead. Assuming that Debra Wert wakes up and can remember."

McDaniel handed Rick a .45 automatic. "A team will move on Gilman Martin and Ultimate Getaways about the same time as we're going in this morning. Maybe we'll get the evidence to tie him to your father's murder." McDaniel handed Rick three ammo magazines for the weapon. "I expect to get the automatic back unused."

McDaniel slammed the trunk. "Tanner got us a name for one of our kidnappers. Bruce Lambert."

As the special agent walked away, Rick separated out the smaller vest. "Here. Let's get you suited up." He slipped it over Jillian's head, tightening the straps. He tapped his knuckles against the steel breastplate. "It'll stop most types of ammunition but not all." He was worrying about her again. Couldn't seem to stop himself. "So don't go playing Superwoman on me, okay? Let the professionals handle it. I plan to."

"So you're okay sitting on the sidelines?"

"I'm okay with it." He wasn't really. His adrenaline had been kicking in pretty hard for the past few minutes, and it was going to be hard sitting in that car next to her just waiting. But at least he knew she would be safe.

When he started to move forward again, she pulled him to a stop by grabbing his arm.

"Thanks, Rick." She didn't release him. "For being there throughout this. For last night."

He didn't know how to respond so settled simply for "You're welcome." He grabbed her hand, wrapped it in his own. "Come on. We're missing the briefing."

He knew she was nervous and frightened. That she'd slept very little. He hadn't slept much more. Partially because his mind had been working overtime, mentally reviewing the floor plans that Sheriff Tanner delivered to Rick's room last night, and partially because he'd been worried about her.

How was she going to take it if the other victims walked out of that house today and there were still no answers about Megan?

And what if that didn't change next week or next year? He'd made a promise to Jillian that he might not be able to keep.

Friday, 6:12 a.m.

THE FACT THAT the temperature hung just below freezing no longer penetrated Jillian's mind. She and Rick had sat in the car for as long as they could—about seven and a half minutes—before they both had climbed out. They now stood next to it, staring at the woods above them.

It had been more than twenty minutes since they'd watched Tanner's deputies and Durwood's agents disappear into the trees, and since then the sky overhead had brightened from a dark, sodden gray to a leaden one that still shed snow.

Jillian assumed that the wood smoke sifting up from the distant trees marked the home's location. How long a hike was it?

She glanced to where Rick paced at the back of the SUV. "How much longer do you think?"

"Depends on what happens when they serve the warrant." He scowled as he shoved his hands into his pockets, hunching his shoulders against the cold.

There was no sign of the automatic weapon McDaniel had supplied, and the protective vest was hidden beneath the leather coat. She wondered if he found it as uncomfortable as she did.

Jillian stamped her feet trying to keep the circulation going. She was coming out of her skin. Even though she knew it was unlikely that Megan was inside the house, there was a part of her that still believed everyone could be wrong. That by some miracle Megan was in that house right now. That Jillian would be able to hug her sister before the morning was over.

Jillian glanced at Rick. Last night he'd held her throughout the night, murmuring words of comfort when the fear in her was so great that it had driven her from sleep.

Could people actually fall in love in a matter of days?

Was she in love with him?

Or when all this was over, would they both walk away without looking back?

She had just glanced toward the trees again when birds exploded from them on silent wings. Then she heard the *pop, pop* of distant gunfire.

Before she had time even to react, Rick was ripping open the nearest door of the SUV and shoving her inside. "Keep the doors locked." He leaned back in. "I'll come back for you as soon as it's safe."

But as she watched him sprinting up into the trees, toward gunfire, she worried that it might be the last time she saw him alive.

Chapter Nineteen

The scent of gunpowder lingered in the luxurious kitchen, somehow at odds with the aroma of sizzling sausage. Stepping over the man he'd just shot, Rick turned off the stove burner and then returned his attention to the dead man just inside the back door.

Having studied the composite and from the description Jillian had given them, he felt fairly certain that he'd just killed the shorter of the two kidnappers.

Leaning over the man, Rick tugged the wallet from the man's back pocket and flipped it open. He thumbed out the driver's license and read the name. Jimmy Young. The address listed was Lexington, Kentucky. Rick checked the rest of the contents of the wallet. Unfortunately, he didn't find anything worthwhile.

Hearing someone behind him, Rick whirled, the .45 coming up. But when he saw Durwood, he immediately lowered the weapon and flicked on the safety.

On his way across the kitchen, the special agent retrieved Young's weapon from where Rick had kicked it, and then squatted to check out the dead man.

"His name's Jimmy Young." Rick passed the wallet. "Any sign of Bruce Lambert?"

"We have three bodies upstairs, two in the basement and four in the garage. Lambert could be among them. I have Carmichael checking it out now."

Letting out a harsh breath, Rick ran a hand through his hair in frustration.

Straightening, Durwood held out his hand. "Better give me your weapon, Brady."

Rick handed him the automatic. "What about Megan? Any sign of her?" If Megan had been sold, if she wasn't among the women locked in the basement, there had been only two people who could lead them to Megan. Rick had just killed one of them, and if Lambert was among the other bodies…

"No. But we have six women in the basement still unconscious and three in a soundproof room upstairs. Once the premises are secure, we'll have Jillian take a look at the ones in the basement. Maybe she'll be able to recognize some of them from Monday night."

The sounds of men pounding up and down staircases continued, as did those of doors being opened and slammed as the house was searched. Durwood's radio went off and Rick listened to Carmichael's transmission.

Durwood lowered the phone. "I guess you heard? Lambert wasn't among the bodies."

The tightness in Rick's chest eased somewhat. As much as he wanted to go search for Lambert, Rick recognized that there were deputies and agents already doing so, that maybe his services were needed elsewhere.

Rick glanced at Durwood. "Where do you need me right now?"

The FBI special agent slid the cell phone into the holder at his waist. "I'm waiting on ambulances for the women and two of Tanner's deputies." Durwood exhaled sharply. "And one of mine is dead." His mouth tightened. "Agent Kennedy and his wife were expecting their first child next month, and now…"

After several seconds Durwood seemed to realize that he wasn't alone, that the job he was there to do hadn't been completed. Still standing over Jimmy Young, Durwood shrugged his shoulders, almost as if unloading some of the weight from them. He lifted his gaze to Rick's. "Have you ever seen a brothel like this one?"

"No."

Durwood turned, scanned the kitchen. "All the amenities of a five-star hotel and then some." He glanced at Rick again. "You're a good man to have around." And then, as if he recalled Rick's earlier offer to help out, he said, "Why don't you go check on Jillian."

As Durwood moved toward the front of the house again, Rick followed him. They'd just reached the foyer when the front door suddenly slammed open and one of Tanner's deputies shoved a man dressed in slacks and a golf shirt through the opening ahead of him.

Behind the deputy and his prisoner, out in the driveway, the first of the ambulances had arrived and the EMTs were dragging a stretcher out the back end.

As Rick refocused on the prisoner, he realized that Jillian had gotten every detail of Bruce Lambert's physical appearance right, even down to his height and coloring—six-two, dark red hair and a light complexion.

Lambert's hands were anchored behind him with zip restraints and it looked as if he'd taken a bullet in his left arm.

"Move it," the deputy ordered, forcing Lambert into the expansive living room and then shoving him onto a straight-backed chair.

The deputy turned to Durwood. "Two of them tried to run up into the mountains. If one of your agents can take care of transporting him, I'll grab a couple deputies and head up into the woods. See if we can't get that other one.

The first set of EMTs hustled in the door as Langley was descending from the second level. He immediately directed them up the stairs and followed them.

Durwood held out the weapon he'd taken from Rick only a few moments earlier. "I need to see about Agent Kennedy's body. Can you keep an eye on Lambert here?"

Rick nodded, but didn't take the gun. "Maybe it's better if you don't give me that."

Rick fully understood that Durwood needed to see to his men and the female victims first. The interrogation of Lambert would come later.

But Rick was thinking about Jillian. He'd left her waiting in the car. She'd trusted him enough to stay behind. And now he was going to have to tell her that they were no closer to finding her sister. That even though she had made the rescue of nine women possible, it was unlikely that her sister would be coming home tonight.

Or maybe ever.

Unless this man talked. And once he lawyered up, his

attorney would make certain that he didn't. Not unless the prosecution offered a deal. Which would be weeks or months away.

"Where is she?" Rick demanded. "The girl that you sold yesterday?"

Lambert shook his head. "I don't know what you're talking about."

Rick got down in his face. "If anything has happened to her…"

"Yeah? What?" The guy looked up at him, grinning. "You're going to hurt me?"

Rick wrapped his hand around the scumbag's upper arm, the one with the bullet wound, and squeezed. "I'm going to do a hell of lot more than hurt you."

Cursing, Lambert looked for someone to complain to. But of course there was no one; they were either on the second floor dealing with the dead or outside searching the grounds.

"I want a lawyer."

"And I want the name of the man you sold her to." Rick tightened his hold on the wounded arm. Sweat popped out on Lambert's face. "And guess who better get what he wants real soon?"

It took every ounce of Rick's control not to act on the urge to slam his fist into the son of a bitch's face. But Rick didn't intend to do anything that would leave physical signs—cuts, bruising or broken bones…

The guy glanced up, still cocky. "Get out of my face. You're nothing. You got nothing to offer me."

Rick stepped back. He was getting nowhere. "Well, Lambert, that's where you're wrong. I do have something to offer you."

"Yeah. Right." The guy winked.

Grabbing the topmost rung of the chair back and a handhold of Lambert's red hair, Rick dragged both the fifteen feet to a closed door. He kicked it open. The room looked like any other office in a high-end home. Lots of dark woods and thick rugs. Expensive furnishings. Everything looked normal until the television was switched to the closed-circuit camera aimed at a bed on the second floor.

"You know why I brought you in here, Lambert?" Rick hauled the chair into the middle of the room, then closed and locked the door.

"You think you're scaring me?" Lambert laughed.

"Not yet." Rick grabbed the trash can next to the desk.

With his back to Rick, Lambert kept turning his head first one direction and then the other, trying to keep track of Rick. Even though Lambert was still talking big, he was nervous.

Rick emptied the can onto the floor, then grabbed the plastic liner. Lambert didn't see it coming. Rick jerked the bag over Lambert's head, wrapping it tightly around his neck.

Lambert threw his weight forward, trying to escape, but Rick held on, using the bag to control him.

After several seconds he pulled the bag off.

"I want a name, Lambert. And if I don't get it in the next five seconds, I'm—"

Lambert's chest heaved. "I don't have one."

Rick shoved the bag over Lambert's head again, held on, this time allowing it to go on a few seconds longer. As soon as Rick pulled off the bag this time, Lambert dragged in air. "An e-mail address. That's how we contacted each other. Through the Internet."

"What is it?"

"I don't know. It's on the laptop. In the van."

Rick stepped around in front of Lambert. "Where was the meet?"

"Three hours south. Route 44. An overlook."

"When?"

"Yesterday around 4:00 p.m." Lambert looked up at Rick. "Guy was driving an old motor home with Maryland plates."

"Was the location prearranged?"

"No. Last minute. He called Jimmy's cell number."

"Open this goddamn door," Durwood yelled as he pounded on the other side of it.

Rick turned back to Lambert. He still needed information and knew as soon as Lambert thought he was out of the woods, he'd shut up fast. "There was no phone on him."

Lambert just stared at him. Obviously he had decided he could stop talking.

Rick jerked the bag back on. "That door looks sturdy to me. You sure you want to gamble on which one will hold out the longest—the door or you?"

This time as soon as the bag came off, Lambert said, "In the van. Sometimes he leaves it in the van."

Rick had just shoved the bag away when Durwood and Langley burst through the door. "Get the hell out of here, Brady!"

Lambert swore. "Police brutality."

"Sorry," Durwood answered. "You're out of luck. The man's not a cop."

Langley hauled Rick out into the other room and toward the front door just as Jillian was coming through it with a deputy. Rick pulled her outside, away from where a team of EMTs was bringing out one of Tanner's deputies. A second team followed. The face staring up this time belonged to a young girl, her blond hair plastered to her skull, her lips nearly blue.

"Do you recognize her?" Rick asked.

Jillian nodded as the EMTs struggled with the stretcher. Her fingers grasped the girl's for the briefest of seconds, then her eyes swung to Rick, asking the one question that Rick didn't want to have to answer.

"Megan?"

He could see the hope in her face and the fear, too. And seeing it was like getting sucker punched.

Rick shook his head. "No."

Turning away, Jillian pressed her fist to her mouth. As much as he wanted to comfort her, there just wasn't time right now. "Come on. I need to find Jimmy Young's cell phone." Taking her by the elbow, he pulled her toward the detached six-car garage.

"Why?"

"Because the man who has Megan called Young's phone yesterday, and it might lead us to Megan."

As they entered the garage, they had to step around two bodies, neither of them law enforcement. The phone was in the center console.

He used Durwood's handkerchief to pick it up. Better not to leave fingerprints that he would have to explain later. There were five calls in the incoming log for the previous day, and only one of them wasn't a local number.

The motor home had Maryland plates, but that didn't necessarily mean the cellular number would have a Maryland area code.

Rick looked up. "Give me your cell phone."

He could have gone back in and given Durwood Jimmy Young's phone, but the man already had enough on his plate. He had ten bodies to deal with, two injured deputies and not enough men.

Besides, if the guy who'd bought Megan had been cautious enough not to give his name and had insisted on choosing the spot for the exchange, he probably had been smart enough to use a throw-away cell phone. They were probably chasing another dead end. But at least he'd be doing something.

Alec Blade answered on the second ring. Rick and Alec had gone to school together, and even though Alec was no longer with the FBI, he had contacts there.

"Do you have a pencil?" Rick asked.

"Whatever happened to saying hello first?"

"I need you to write down some phone numbers for me. And then I need you to check out one of them for me. If it's not a throw-away cell phone, I need a name. And if it is a throw-away and it's still active, I need a location."

For several seconds there was silence on the other end, and Rick wondered if Alec was going to turn him down.

"What's this about?"

"I don't have time to go into that right now."

Another long pause. "Give me your number. I'll see what I can do."

As soon as he hung up, Rick put the phone back where he found it. If anything came of the lead, Rick would contact Durwood or Langley and have them retrieve it. Otherwise the phone would be collected when the van was processed.

"Is he going to do it?"

"Yeah. Come on. I was officially kicked off the property five minutes ago."

"Why? What happened?"

"Let's just say that I got carried away. And that it's a damned good thing that I'm not a cop."

They were on the way back to the hotel when Alec phoned. Rick whipped the SUV off the road.

"Got something to write with?" Alec asked.

Rick grabbed the map from above the visor and a pen from the console. "The phone is a throw-away, purchased two days ago."

"Is it active?"

"Yeah. I have the GPS coordinates for you."

Rick wrote them down as they were read off. "Any idea where that is?"

"Just east of New Carlyle, Pennsylvania."

Even as Alec was saying it, Rick was jumping out of the car, racing to the back end to grab his duffel bag. Throwing it into Jillian's lap, he dropped the SUV back into gear.

"What's going on?" Jillian caught the bag, settled it across her knees.

"The man who has Megan is here in New Carlyle." He took his eyes off the road. "Open up the bag. There's a handheld GPS in there. Get it."

When she had it in her hands, he swerved into the next driveway and punched in the coordinates, then pulled out onto the road again.

"Now call Langley. Give him those coordinates. Tell him to meet us there and that he's most likely looking for a motor home with Maryland plates."

Rick ran it all through his head. If the exchange had taken place three hours south at 4:00 p.m. yesterday, what was the guy doing here in New Carlyle?

Chapter Twenty

Time unknown

Megan heard him coming even before he dragged her off the bed and onto the floor. He hadn't turned on any lights, but a small amount entered through the windshield, filtering to the back of the motor home, backlighting him. He had the massive neck and shoulders of a weight lifter.

Was this it? Had they reached their destination? Her breathing turned shallow and fast. Was he going to rape her now?

"Get up."

She didn't move. Couldn't make her muscles respond. She had never understood the term "paralyzed with fear" until that moment.

When she remained frozen, he reached down for her. Screaming, she tried to scramble backward, but of course there was no place to go in the tight quarters.

"Shut up," he ordered, his fingers twisting into the cotton fabric of her dress. He towed her to the tiny bathroom and shoved her into the shower. He left her for several seconds. When he came back, he covered her mouth with duct tape. "Don't try anything. I'm going to be right outside." He grabbed her chin roughly. "You understand? You try anything, and I'll kill you."

The only response she could manage was a harsh intake of breath.

As the bathroom door banged shut, she closed her eyes, tried to focus only on the sounds coming through it. He was digging in drawers again. Why? What was he looking for?

The stench of the motor home's holding tank overpowered that of the mildew and she gagged. Her hands had gone numb hours ago, and her shoulders ached from the unnatural position.

He'd said he was going to be outside. But was that just to scare her? To keep her from attempting to escape?

When the exterior door slammed a few minutes later, everything went relatively silent. Trapped in the dark, she continued to listen. A sharp wind buffeted the motor home, causing it to rock slightly. As the breeze died down, the vehicle would settle into stillness until the next gust came along. The soft scraping sound was probably just a branch against the metal siding. There was nothing to suggest that anyone was just outside.

But what if she was wrong? Would he really kill her? Should she wait for another opportunity? What if there wasn't one? What if this was her only chance and she lost it because she was too damn scared to act?

Even as she squirmed out of the shower and onto the bathroom floor, her heart thundered with fear. Shifting so that her feet were against the door, she drew them back and let fly. It took three tries before the door exploded open.

Megan had made it as far as the kitchen floor and was struggling to get onto her feet so that she could check the drawers for a knife when the exterior door was suddenly jerked open. Accompanied by frigid air, he bounded up into the motor home and came to a sudden halt. "What the hell!"

Closing her eyes, Megan waited for the blow, but it never came. Instead he grabbed her as he had the last time, using a handful of cotton dress to drag her to the bed.

He hefted her up on the mattress. "And this is the thanks I get for saving your ass. I should never have gotten involved. I've got enough damn problems."

He rolled her onto her stomach and checked the duct-tape bindings. "Damn cops. They're swarming everywhere. They're going to screw it up again. I'll never get her back."

What was he talking about?

Get who back?

Friday, 8:42 a.m.

JILLIAN'S HEART was racing as Rick pulled the SUV in behind some trees. They'd driven by the narrow lane once already, and from their current position, they could just make out the entrance to it.

"This is close enough for now," Rick said. "Tanner should be here soon. We'll sit tight until then."

Jillian's hand crept toward the door handle. What if he was hurting her sister right now? And she was this close and did nothing to stop it? Fear tightened her chest. What if Tanner didn't arrive in time? What if the guy somehow managed to get away? They'd never find him. She'd never get Megan back.

Jillian was out of the car before Rick could stop her. She nearly lost her footing as she scrambled into the woods. Almost immediately Rick was crashing after her. Hearing an engine turn over, she changed direction, dodging pine trees and saplings as she ran toward the sound.

One second she was in the trees and the next she was standing in the middle of a snow-covered lane, the motor home heading straight for her.

For a moment she was paralyzed, the sense of déjà vu so strong that it kept her motionless. And then, at the last second, the driver jerked the wheel, sending them into the side ditch.

The man leaped out. "Are you nuts? I could have killed you!"

Jillian pushed past him and into the motor home.

She found Megan on the floor next to the bed. Leaving the duct tape in place, Jillian grabbed her sister and staggered toward the door.

The man had followed her in and now blocked the door.

"Get out of my way!"

One moment the man was there and the next Rick had grabbed him from behind, dragging him outside. The guy came up swinging even as Jillian ripped the tape off Megan's mouth.

"No!" Megan screamed. "Don't hurt him. He's trying to save his sister. They have her. She's in another van."

Friday, 10:19 a.m.

JILLIAN PACED in front of where Megan was perched on the edge of a bed in Carlyle County Hospital's emergency room. They were waiting for a doctor to stitch up the gash on the side of Megan's head.

There was activity all around them—a nurse rustled by, pushing a cart with medical equipment on it, a doctor held up a large X-ray film so that he could read it, another patient shuffled past cradling a portable oxygen tank in her arms. But the silence in the curtained-off area where Jillian and Megan waited hung heavy.

A silence that Jillian didn't know how to breach.

"It shouldn't be much longer," Jillian offered, and sank onto the chair next to the bed.

When the door between the emergency room and the waiting area opened moments later, Jillian glanced up. Rick stood in the opening. As their gazes met, the tightness in her chest eased, and she realized she was smiling for the first time in five days.

"I just heard from Durwood. The second van arrived about forty-five minutes ago. The women are safe."

When the task force had learned that another vehicle carrying captives was due to arrive at the compound, they had quickly cleared the area, leaving only a few officers behind inside the home and several more scattered in the trees just inside the entrance gates.

Megan looked up. "Sam's....Sam's sister. Was she one of them?"

"Yes," Rick said. "And she's fine."

As Rick retreated to the waiting area again, Megan looked over at Jillian. "He seems nice."

Jillian nodded. "Yeah." But even as she said it, the smile faded from her lips. Last night, instead of one hotel room, Rick had gotten two, and instead of making love to her, he'd just held her in his arms. And then today he'd barely touched her.

Was it because he hadn't wanted to make assumptions where their relationship was concerned, or because he regretted what had occurred between them over the past few days and was trying to let her down easily? Was that what was happening?

Glancing at Megan, Jillian realized she shouldn't even be thinking about Rick, about a man she'd known for less than five days. Her sister had been through hell. That's where Jillian's focus needed to be. With Megan.

So far Jillian had refrained from asking anything about Megan's ordeal, but there would come a time when they would have to deal with it. For now it was enough to have her sister safe.

Megan stared at her hands. "They killed her?" She lifted her gaze. "The woman we were trying to save that night." Megan lowered her chin again.

"No." Jillian got up and crossed to the bed, sitting next to Megan as she had so many times over the years, offering comfort, sharing secrets. She wrapped Megan's left hand in her own. "No. She's alive."

"But I saw…" For the first time since she'd been rescued, Megan's eyes filled with tears. "They made me watch them bury her."

Jillian turned and wrapped her arms around her sister. "They may have left her for dead, but she survived."

Jillian tightened her embrace. "We have all survived."

Chapter Twenty-One

Three weeks later, 9:30 p.m.

Jillian glanced at the diners at the other tables, then her gaze swept to the mob waiting near the entrance. Charlie's was one of the city's best restaurants, so she suspected there was always a line to get in, especially on a Friday.

She was taking another sip of champagne when she saw him at the back of the crowd—a man wearing a Western hat. Jillian lowered the glass flute and, with her heart slamming hard behind her ribs, started to rise. But by the time she reached her feet, she'd lost sight of him.

She'd been doing that a lot recently. Searching crowds for Western hats. For tall, handsome men. For Rick Brady.

But he was never there.

As Jillian sank back down, Megan broke off her conversation with Debra Wert and glanced over her shoulder in the direction Jillian had been looking. "What is it?"

Jillian reached for her glass again. "Nothing. I just thought I saw someone."

Megan's eyes narrowed. "Who?"

"No one."

"First it's someone and then it's no one?" Megan grinned as she topped off Jillian's champagne. "Drink up. This is supposed to be a party."

The first bottle had arrived with their appetizers, the second sometime during the entrée. Jillian had ordered the third to go with the dessert she wasn't having.

Obediently she picked up her glass. The restaurant was the perfect spot for a celebration. They'd already witnessed two birthdays and a fiftieth wedding anniversary.

And even if Jillian wasn't feeling in the mood for it, there was much to commemorate. Gilman Martin was behind bars and awaiting trial for both white slavery and the murder of Rick's father. Megan would be starting medical school after the first of the year and Jillian had accepted a position with a small family-law practice. And perhaps the best reason of all was Debra's recent release the hospital.

Jillian glanced at the two women across from her. Megan and Debra were deep in conversation again. They had become unbelievably close, and there were times recently when the three of them had been together that Jillian had felt like the outsider, as if her place in Megan's life had been usurped by Debra—which was damned ridiculous.

The only real low spot in Jillian's life was that she hadn't seen Rick since that day at the hospital, hadn't heard from him in nearly a week now. And whenever he phoned, it had always been to update her on the investigation, or to inform her of indictments as they were handed down. Never once had they discussed what had taken place between them during those four days.

And maybe if her heart hadn't been slowly splintering into a million pieces, she could have lived with that. It wasn't as if she wanted to need him, or even to love him.

But the truth was that even if she never saw him, if he never held her in his arms again, it wouldn't change how she felt about him.

She was in love with Rick Brady—and damned well didn't know what to do about it.

She finished off the champagne in one long swallow and then considered an age-old question—whether to continue drowning her sorrows or embrace her blessings. But when she glanced at the champagne bucket, she realized the bottle had been upended in the ice. Time to call it a night.

Five minutes later she left Megan and Debra sitting in the lounge talking to Langley, who had come in as they were leaving.

As Jillian walked toward the exterior door, she found herself scanning the faces of people she passed, looking for one in particular.

Stepping outside into the brisk night, Jillian handed her claim stub to the parking attendant. As she was waiting for her new convertible to be brought around, a slow-moving horse carriage drawn by a large chestnut with white socks approached. The attendant wore a black hat—a black top hat.

Carriages were a common sight in Charleston, but

whenever Jillian saw one, she thought about her mother. Not the one she'd shared with Megan, but the one who had given birth to her, who had filled the first five years of her life with love.

Jillian had been afraid to come home to Charleston, to face the ghosts of her past. But she now embraced them. Without the dark moments in her life, she wouldn't understand just how fortunate she was.

When the carriage drew even with her, it stopped. She glanced up at the driver, intending to tell him that she wasn't interested, but then heard a familiar voice just behind her.

"Come take a ride with me," Rick said. She whirled to face him, recalling the night they'd made love in the backseat of a car. When they had been each other's *firsts*.

She didn't want that to be the only first they shared. She wanted so many more. She wanted to share a first anniversary with him. Wanted to carry his first child. Wanted to watch the first steps of their child with Rick right there beside her. And then she realized that more than all those firsts, what she really wanted was to be his *last*—the woman he could never let go of.

Her chest tightened as he removed his hat and held it in front of him. She wanted so much to throw herself into his arms, but they weren't open for her.

"All right," she managed, fighting the lump in her throat.

Turning, she allowed the driver to help her up. Rick climbed in after her, sat facing her.

Neither of them said anything for several minutes as the carriage melded into the line of slow-moving cars. Christmas lights winked in the trees. The breeze carried the scent of the nearby water. The tinkle of a Salvation Army bell could be heard somewhere close by.

As they moved out of the crowded downtown area and into the tranquility of side streets, her heart raced ahead of the rhythmic clip-clop of the horse's hooves.

Jillian was the first to speak. "When I was a little girl, if I was really good, my mom—my real mom—would take me down to the carriage stables so I could see the horses up close. I'd choose which one I liked best. I'd always rename him Prince, and she would always promise that we'd go for a ride someday."

"Did you?" Rick asked quietly.

"No. And years later I decided that I was glad we hadn't."

"Why?" He tossed the hat onto the seat next to her.

"Because if we had gone on a carriage ride, I wouldn't think about the trips to the stables or all the moments we shared as I talked nonsense about a bunch of horses and dreamed about something that even I knew wasn't going to happen. All I would have to remember is a single Sunday carriage ride."

She had never told that to anyone, not even Megan. What was it about this man that made her want to open up? To share parts of herself that she'd kept hidden for so many years?

She glanced at the house they were passing, at the lighted Christmas tree in the front window and the poinsettias lining the brick stairs.

"Marry me, Jillian."

She looked at Rick, trying to read his face as she ran his words through her numb mind a second time. Had he just asked her to marry him? Was that possible?

As the carriage rolled to a stop, Rick's hands caught hers. He stood, dragging her from the seat and into his arms. "Marry me, Jillian."

As their gazes met, she realized that among the many *firsts* she'd listed, she'd overlooked at least one.

"I love you, Rick. And I've never said that to another man."

Welcome to cowboy country...

Turn the page for a sneak preview of
TEXAS BABY
by
Kathleen O'Brien
An exciting new title from
Harlequin Superromance
for everyone who loves
stories about the West.

Harlequin Superromance—
Where life and love weave together in
emotional and unforgettable ways.

CHAPTER ONE

CHASE TRANSFERRED his gaze to the road and identified a foreign spot on the horizon. A car. Almost half a mile away, where the straight, tree-lined drive met the public road. He could tell it was coming too fast, but judging the speed of a vehicle moving straight toward you was tricky.

It wasn't until it was about two hundred yards away that he realized the driver must be drunk…or crazy. Or both.

The guy was going maybe sixty. On a private drive, out here in ranch country, where kids or horses or tractors or stupid chickens might come darting out any minute, that was criminal. Chase straightened from his comfortable slouch and waved his hands.

"Slow down, you fool," he called out. He took the porch steps quickly and began walking fast down the driveway.

The car veered oddly, from one lane to another, then up onto the slight rise of the thick green spring grass. It just barely missed the fence.

"Slow down, damn it!"

He couldn't see the driver, and he didn't recognize this

automobile. It was small and old, and couldn't have cost much even when it was new. It was probably white, but now it needed either a wash or a new paint job or both.

"Damn it, what's wrong with you?"

At the last minute, he had to jump away, because the idiot behind the wheel clearly wasn't going to turn to avoid a collision. He couldn't believe it. The car kept coming, finally slowing a little, but it was too late.

Still going about thirty miles an hour, it slammed into the large, white-brick pillar that marked the front boundaries of the house. The pillar wasn't going to give an inch, so the car had to. The front end folded up like a paper fan.

It seemed to take forever for the car to settle, as if the trauma happened in slow motion, reverberating from the front to the back of the car in ripples of destruction. The front windshield suddenly seemed to ice over with lethal bits of glassy frost. Then the side windows exploded.

The front driver's door wrenched open, as if the car wanted to expel its contents. Metal buckled hideously. Small pieces, like hubcaps and mirrors, skipped and ricocheted insanely across the oyster-shell driveway.

Finally, everything was still. Into the silence, a plume of steam shot up like a geyser, smelling of rust and heat. Its snakelike hiss almost smothered the low, agonized moan of the driver.

Chase's anger had disappeared. He didn't feel anything but a dull sense of disbelief. Things like this didn't happen in real life. Not in his life. Maybe the sun had actually put him to sleep....

But he was already kneeling beside the car. The driver was a woman. The frosty glass-ice of the windshield was dotted with small flecks of blood. She must have hit it with her head, because just below her hairline a red liquid was seeping out. He touched it. He tried to wipe it away before it reached her eyebrow, though of course, that made no sense at all. Her eyes were shut.

Was she conscious? Did he dare move her? Her dress was covered in glass, and the metal of the car was sticking out lethally in all the wrong places.

Then he remembered, with an intense relief, that every good medical man in the county was here, just behind the house, drinking his champagne. He found his phone and paged Trent.

The woman moaned again.

Alive, then. Thank God for that.

He saw Trent coming toward him, starting out at a lope, but quickly switching to a full run.

"Get Dr. Marchant," Chase called. "Don't bother with 911."

Trent didn't take long to assess the situation. A fraction of a second, and he began pulling out his cell phone and running toward the house.

The yelling seemed to have roused the woman. She opened her eyes. They were blue and clouded with pain and confusion.

"Chase," she said.

His breath stalled. His head pulled back. "What?"

Her only answer was another moan, and he wondered if he had imagined the word. He reached around her and put his arm behind her shoulders. She was tiny. Probably petite by nature, but surely way too thin. He could feel her shoulder blades pushing against her skin, as fragile as the wishbone in a turkey.

She seemed to have passed out, so he put his other arm under her knees and lifted her out. He tried to avoid the jagged metal, but her skirt caught on a piece and the tearing sound seemed to wake her again.

"No," she said. "Please."

"I'm just trying to help," he said. "It's going to be all right."

She seemed profoundly distressed. She wriggled in his arms, and she was so weak, like a broken bird. It made him feel too big and brutish. And intrusive. As if touching her this way, his bare hands against the warm skin behind her knees, were somehow a transgression.

He wished he could be more delicate. But he smelled gasoline, and he knew it wasn't safe to leave her here.

Finally he heard the sound of voices, as guests began to run around the side of the house, alerted by Trent. Dr. Marchant was at the front, racing toward them as if he were forty instead of seventy. Susannah was right behind him, her green dress floating around her trim legs.

"Please," the woman in his arms murmured again. She looked at him, the expression in her blue eyes lost and bewildered. He wondered if she might be on drugs. Hitting her head on the windshield might account for this unfocused, glazed look, but it couldn't explain the crazy driving.

"Please, put me down. Susannah... The wedding..."

Chase's arms tightened instinctively, and he froze in

his tracks. She whimpered, and he realized he might be hurting her. "Say that again?"

"The wedding. I have to stop it."

* * * * *

Be sure to look for TEXAS BABY,
available September 11, 2007,
as well as other fantastic Superromance titles
available in September.

HARLEQUIN®

Mediterranean NIGHTS™

Experience glamour, elegance, mystery and revenge aboard the high seas....

Coming in September 2007...

BREAKING ALL THE RULES

by

Marisa Carroll

Aboard the cruise ship *Alexandra's Dream* for some R & R, sports journalist Lola Sandler is surprised to spot pro-golfer Eric Lashman. Years after walking away from the pro circuit with no explanation to the public, Eric now finds himself teaching aboard a cruise ship.

Lola smells a career-making exposé... but their developing relationship may force her to make a difficult choice.

HM38963

Bailey DelMonico has finally
gotten her life on track, and is
passionate about her recent career
change. Nothing will stand in the way
of her becoming a doctor…that is,
until she's paired with the sharp-tongued
Dr. Ivan Munro.

Watch the sparks fly in

Doctor in
the House

by *USA TODAY* Bestselling Author
Marie Ferrarella

Available September 2007

Intrigued? Read more at
TheNextNovel.com

HARLEQUIN®
Next™

ATHENA FORCE

Heart-pounding romance and thrilling adventure.

Professional negotiator Lindsey Novak is faced with her biggest challenge—to buy back Teal Arnett, a young woman with unique powers. In the process Lindsey uncovers a devastating plot that involves scientists from around the globe, and all of them lead to one woman who is bent on destroying Athena Academy…at any cost.

LOOK FOR

THE GOOD THIEF

by Judith Leon

Available September wherever you buy books.

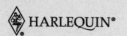# HARLEQUIN®

INTRIGUE®

COMING NEXT MONTH

#1011 RESTLESS WIND by Aimée Thurlo
Brotherhood of Warriors
Entrusted with the secrets of the Brotherhood of Warriors, Dana Seles must aid Ranger Blueeyes to prevent the secret Navajo order from extinction.

#1012 MEET ME AT MIDNIGHT by Jessica Andersen
Lights Out (Book 4 of 4)
On what was to be their first date, Secret Service agent Ty Jones and Gabriella Solano have only hours to rescue the kidnapped vice president.

#1013 INTIMATE DETAILS by Dana Marton
Mission: Redemption
On a mission to recover stolen WMDs, Gina Torno is caught by Cal Spencer. Do they have conflicting orders or is each just playing hard to get?

#1014 BLOWN AWAY by Elle James
After an American embassy bombing, T. J. Barton thought new love Sean McNeal died in the explosion. But when he reappears, T.J. and Sean must shadow the country's most powerful citizens in order to stop a high-class conspiracy.

#1015 NINE-MONTH PROTECTOR by Julie Miller
The Precinct: Vice Squad
After Sarah Cartwright witnesses a mob murder, it's up to Detective Cooper Bellamy to protect her—and her unborn child. But has he crossed the line in falling for his best friend's sister?

#1016 BODYGUARD CONFESSIONS by Donna Young
When the royal palace of Taer is attacked, Quamar Bazan Al Asadi begins a desperate race across the Sahara with presidential daughter Anna Cambridge and a five-month-old royal heir. Can they restore order before the rebels close in?

www.eHarlequin.com